THREE OF A KIND

"Deal 'em then," the cowboy said.

Joe Tony shuffled, cut and dealt. The game resumed; the other players remained silent, intent on their own cards.

Slocum saw Joe Tony's eyes flicker as his right arm tightened and he leaned forward with his hands beneath the table.

"You're a lying sonofabitch, a goddam cheat!" His words landed like bullets in the waiting room.

And then Slocum saw it. They must have forgotten the mirror, the fools, for it was there he saw the man in the black shirt come in with his two partners. Some sixth sense had ignited the entire saloon, for men had hit the floor; others had thrown themselves out of the range of fire. The three visitors drew . . .

OTHER BOOKS BY JAKE LOGAN

JAKE LOGAN

SLOCUM AND THE
HANGING PARTY

BERKLEY BOOKS, NEW YORK

SLOCUM AND THE HANGING PARTY

A Berkley Book / published by arrangement with
the author

PRINTING HISTORY
Berkley edition / September 1991

ISBN: 0-425-12904-7

A BERKLEY BOOK® TM 757,375
Berkley Books are published by The Berkley Publishing Group,
200 Madison Avenue, New York, New York 10016.
The name "BERKLEY" and the "B" logo
are trademarks belonging to Berkley Publishing Corporation.

PRINTED IN THE UNITED STATES OF AMERICA

10 9 8 7 6 5 4 3 2 1

1

The moment he heard the gunshots, John Slocum rode the Appaloosa off the trail. Although the sound of the firing hadn't been that close, he wasn't taking any chances. He'd trailed a rough herd up from Texas to Ogallala where he'd delivered the three thousand head of brush cattle, and he was still on the sharp edge of his vigilance as he headed farther north toward the Arapaho-Cheyenne country.

That morning, long shut of the cattle drive, he had ridden under the vast sky of heavy, unbroken clouds. At high noon, the sky had turned blue, revealing the staring disc of the sun, its rays hot on his back and on the knuckles of his bare hands.

He rode up to the edge of the big escarpment, reined the Appaloosa, and stepped down onto the hot buffalo grass. Groundhitching his pony, he took out his field glasses, and found a good place where he would be covered, yet able to sweep the wide valley and river below. He could still hear the gunfire.

It was late spring and the buffalo grass was already

brown, dry, and almost brittle; the land below him lay like a great carpet sweeping toward the river and then up the far side to the giant rimrocks that formed part of the enclosure of the long valley. There was no sign of habitation below, and he put down the field glasses, giving a slight nod, as though in agreement with some thought.

It was then he realized that his eye had caught something. Quickly, he lifted the glasses, and trained them on the far side of the valley.

Except for the breathing of his horse, there was silence, and yet there, far below, he saw the racing stagecoach with its driver whipping his team to its greatest efforts, while the half-dozen galloping riders pursued, firing vigorously. He couldn't quite hear the gunfire now, as the grim scene moved farther toward the horizon; yet he could feel the desperation of that tense, aggressive moment.

The horsebackers were clearly gaining on the stage now. Suddenly, the guard, who had been firing back at the pursuers, rose up as though driven by a blow, his rifle spilling out of his hands, and in the next instant he followed after, as the coach lurched dangerously and looked to Slocum as though about to capsize, yet righting itself as it sped on. The driver was no longer lashing his team; he was holding on for his life.

In the next moment, the stagecoach disappeared into a thick stand of pines, barely able to hold the trail as it paralleled the river.

To Slocum's surprise, the attackers drew rein; the lead rider threw his arm high in the air, while the group of six momentarily disappeared in the sheet of dust raised by their arrested horses.

Why hadn't they continued to pursue the coach? Slocum wondered as he readjusted the glasses, careful that the sunlight wouldn't strike them and give him away. It seemed that they were more interested in the man who'd been riding shotgun than in the coach, its cargo, or its passengers.

The guard had clearly been wounded, and surely shaken up as a result of his plunge from the top of the coach, but he was alive, and Slocum could see he even tried to put up some fight. A tough one, that was sure, and Slocum felt for him. It was a job that gave little thanks and poor pay; and being a hero didn't net you a damn thing but more than likely extra lead. Slocum knew the drill on that one.

He lowered the glasses, listening, and even turning to look down his back trail. He'd be foolish indeed if he allowed someone to slip up on him while he was viewing all the action below. But his trail was clear, and now he resumed his watch.

Below, the riders had all dismounted save for one, who was evidently the leader. At any rate, it was he who was pointing, waving, and standing up in his stirrups like some general. He was a big man, and Slocum figured he had a loud voice, though he couldn't hear it.

Two men had now pulled the wounded shotgun rider to his feet, and it looked to Slocum like they were handling him roughly. The man on horseback pointed toward the cottonwoods along the bank of the river. Slocum noticed that he appeared even bigger than at first. He wore a big Stetson hat, pulled low on his head, and he had only one suspender holding up his trousers, running from near his right hip across to his left shoulder and down the back.

Slocum figured him for a farmer who must have found that running guns and gunslingers was more profitable than growing potatoes. He suddenly remembered hearing of those midwestern farmers who were so poor they wore only one suspender; but that, as a result of that poverty, they were tougher than most, almost a breed apart. Indeed, the man was obviously the leader, not just in his actions, but in the way he sat his horse, handled him, in the very arrogance of his posture. He was now directing his men to do something with a lariat that one of them had taken from his saddle rig. The leader's impatience was clear as he grabbed the rope and began building a knot. In a moment, he tossed the rope back to the man from whom he'd snatched it; tossed it hard. The scene certainly told something about the leader, Slocum reflected.

More instructions were given, and the man with the rope walked to the river's edge and squatting, held the manila lariat under the water.

Now it became clear to Slocum what they were going to do. He felt his guts tighten. He had heard of this particularly cruel style of lynching, and he anticipated the next procedures.

The noose was now slipped over the prisoner's head, the other end of the wet rope thrown over the limb of a nearby tree. Meanwhile, the victim's hands had been tied behind his back and a gag was stuffed in his mouth. But the rope was only pulled just enough to take up the slack. He was not lifted off his feet. He would wait there then, while the rope dried and shortened, and thus he would be hanged.

Slocum watched the men mount up and ride off fast toward the western horizon. He waited; it would take a while for the rope to dry out. There was still time to ride down and free the man. He waited another moment, and then rose and mounted the Appaloosa and quartered down to the river and the man waiting to be lynched.

It was a distance down to where the action had taken place, and the trail was steep, but Slocum was also taking care not to be spotted by any of those wild riders who might be looking over their back trail. He took advantage of every bit of cover, which wasn't much. At the same time, he realized that the perpetrators of this particular kind of lynching would not be overly concerned about checking the result. There was no way the victim could escape either his death or the horrible ordeal of waiting for its certainty.

The captive was, to be sure, still standing. Slocum was surprised to find the noose not really snug about his scrawny neck. He could see right away how weak the man was, and that he was also in pain. Not to mention anger.

"Those sonsofbitch bastards!" The words rasped out of his tight, dry throat the instant Slocum removed the gag.

He was a man of older years. A man typical of his job, shotgun rider: tough, ornery, reliable, with a sulphuric tongue he took obvious delight in using.

"Them fuckers!"

"Where's that stage heading?" Slocum asked as he worked on the knot.

"Bounty. Bountyville."

"How far?"

"Couple, three hours if they ain't delayed more."

Slocum slipped the noose over the man's head, then undid his hands which to his surprise, were not bound as tightly as he expected. Indeed, the captive had almost worked himself loose. "Take it easy moving those arms."

"Wasn't fixin' to go walkin' 'crost the river on 'em."

And Slocum found himself looking into the brightest pair of vinegary blue eyes he'd about ever seen.

" 'Scuse me for breathing, mister," Slocum retorted with an equally sharp dash of vinegar.

The old man suddenly drew back the corners of his mouth and cackled. "Shit take it, young feller. I do 'preciate your comin' by. But now I need to get me to Bounty."

"Bountyville?"

"That's what I just said, didn't I."

Slocum didn't argue the point.

"We'll make it to Bounty then," Slocum said, still sizing up the leathery, waspish, gaunted old geezer who stood there in bib overalls, sucking his gums in between the few teeth that were revealed when he'd cackled.

The old boy canted his head now, sniffed, suddenly scratched deep into his right armpit, then put his hand on his crotch, as though for some sort of inner support. He spat vigorously at a small lizard near his left foot.

"We kin make 'er; 'ceptin' I got no hoss."

"I have."

"Obliged."

Slocum cut his eye fast to detect insincerity in that response, but the old-timer looked as beatific as a professional angel.

"What about that shoulder?" Slocum said, nodding to the bloodstained side of the other's shirt. The shotgunner had pulled a big red bandanna out of his hip pocket and was now holding it in place.

"Nicked me," he said.

"The way you got off that stage it looked like you'd been gutshot," Slocum said.

"If I was, then I never feeled nothin'," said his companion. "Lost my balance."

Slocum wanted to ask why the attackers had been after him, and not the stage, but he decided to wait.

"You got a name?" he asked.

"Sure do." And he looked right at the man who had saved his life as though he didn't give a good or a bad damn about a thing. Slocum liked that. But he said nothing.

Suddenly the old man spoke. "Name's Tyrone."

"Huh," Slocum said, getting even, and feeling good for the opportunity.

"Gulley Tyrone. Yourn'?"

"Slocum."

At that, Gulley Tyrone sniffed, lifted his wiry eyebrows—they looked a bit like horns, Slocum thought—and again canted his gray, bony head at Slocum, drawing a bead with one eye.

"Slocum, you said?"

"That's what I said." Something in the other man's attitude brought some steel into Slocum's words. "You got an objection?"

"Nope. Wouldn't be John Slocum would it? I heerd of you."

The iron-colored eyebrows had lifted, the lips pursed, a mid-distant look appeared in the blue eyes. Innocent as a new whistle, Slocum reflected. Something was up, but he didn't answer the old boy's question.

"Listen, Gulley. I just saved your ass, and risked getting my own self an invitation like yours. Now you come clean with me. Why are you looking so all-fired cockeyed when I tell you my name?"

"Reckon I do owe you," the old man allowed. "Just that name stopped me for a minute. See, there's a Slocum right in Bounty. Slocum—that's a name you don't hear much more than almost never; 'cept it bein' the same person. Like yourself is what I'm meanin'."

"What's his first name?" Slocum asked.

"That's just what I'm saying, Goddamn it. His first name is John. Like yourn', I be wagerin'. John. Huh! You maybe a relative or somethin'? I recollect seein' you oncet anyways. Know I shouldn't be sayin' that, but you just saved my ass, by God." Gulley sucked his few teeth vigorously as he took in the situation, and he scratched himself with his hands deep in his baggy pockets. He seemed to have recovered from his misadventure with the bandits about as much as he was going to; at least as near as Slocum could see.

Slocum said, "What's this fellow in Bounty look like? You know anything about him?"

"Never seen him. Heard about him. I do believe he's one of the vigilantes bunch. Like them that hit the coach."

"Vigilantes?"

"Yup. Regulators, they calls theirselves. That's what Bountyville come to." He wagged his head and spat, turning his head elaborately to do so, then winced with pain and cursed his attackers again.

Evidently feeling Slocum's green eyes probing him, Gulley said, "I got nothin' more to say, mister. Slocum, that is. I do 'preciate you findin' me and endin' what would of bin the end of my life. I reckon—like I said— I owe you somethin'. And that is for sure!" Then he started to cackle, his mouth wide open, revealing brown stubs and spaces where there were no teeth at all, a pretty strong odor of stale tobacco and spittle emerging.

"Want to tell me why they were after you?" Slocum said.

"No, I don't." But then, seeing the look that swept into Slocum's eyes, he bent his head—carefully this time—spat again, and said. "Shit, that's the damn trouble of gettin' rescued from yer own hangin'. You ends up owin' somebody. Shit take it! Shit take it to hell!"

"I'm listening," Slocum said. "Matter of fact—" And he reached over and put his hand on the Appaloosa's neck. "I might even put it that it's a long walk to Bountyville, and—"

"I was just about to tell you what happened," Gulley said. And he ran the back of his wrist over his nose a couple of times to handle the sudden itching.

"You can tell me while we ride," Slocum said. "We've been here too long already."

In another moment, they were up on the Appaloosa, Slocum ordering Gulley to sit in the saddle, while he rode the saddle skirt just behind the cantle. The horse had taken an extra step when Slocum got up on him, adjusting himself to the extra weight. The old man was cursing his sore shoulder and arm, and saying how he could "just as lief walk," but Slocum told him to stop talking so much and save his strength.

But the old boy liked to argue. "Reckon it'd be better for myself to ride behind," he said, making another stab with his orneriness. "You'd be able to handle this here hoss better bein' in the saddle. We'd best swap."

"Shut up," Slocum said, and touched his heels to the Appaloosa.

Gulley sniffed, working up his chew, ready to spit, then turned his head to face downwind and let fly a big gob. "Kind of them boys to leave me my chew," he observed. "Shows a man the world ain't all that cruel like some say."

They rode in silence for several minutes. Suddenly, the old man made a strange sound, like he had a pain, and he started to swear.

"You got something?" Slocum asked, drawing rein.

"Reckon I ain't as young as I useter be. This here is hurtin' some. But I'm good enough. Let's keep goin'."

"You could ride back here and we'll tie you on."

"The hell you say! Told you I was all right. I was only sayin' I was feelin' kind of weak."

"You lost some blood."

"That's what I know. Made me dizzy some. But I'm good now. Hell, I wouldn't say such a thing like about feelin' weak to another man on the face of the earth 'ceptin' John Slocum."

"Cut that out; we got a long ride, and what about that Slocum you mentioned, the one riding with the vigilantes? You sure who you're talking to?"

Slocum heard Gulley's breath whistle as he got ready to speak. "I am sure. Ever since I seen you outdraw and outshoot that smartass Tole Freewiley in Klamath Falls this good while ago. I ain't forgot that!" And he let out a cackle like a horny old rooster sighting his prey.

2

The drive north had been a rough one, and Slocum was glad to be shut of it. As trail boss, he'd had a dozen men under him plus a horse wrangler and a cook. The steers were from three to six years old; brush cattle. Tough. Some hadn't seen more than a couple of men since they'd been small calves, and then only when they had been branded.

The cattle had been bought range delivery the fall before, and they were prime stock; for horses, Slocum had picked some of the toughest and meanest he'd run into in some good while. With those tough beeves, it was necessary to have a mount you could count on. With the Appaloosa included, he found he was riding a top saddle string. It had taken two weeks of steady riding before they started the drive to get the cavvy bridle-wise, and another two weeks to get them where they would turn after a cow.○

Then it had been tough work rounding up the brush cattle. The beeves would lie around in the brush and canebrakes in the daytime and feed at night. And they'd been scattered all over a couple of Texas counties. Luckily, there were a number of dry cows that had previously been driven to mix in with the wild brush animals. Finally, all the cattle had been branded, and Slocum had even taken on extra men until the herd had been trail broken.

The first few days he'd ordered the cattle to be pushed hard, driving them thirty miles a day so that come nightfall they were too tired to give much trouble. Gradually, as they became road broken, he ordered the pace slackened to some dozen miles a day. He had to be careful that the beeves would not arrive north all gaunted and underweight.

Yes, it had been a long, long drive.

It turned out that when they arrived at Dodge City and delivered the steers to their new owners, Slocum was informed that, while the cows had been sold and paid for in Dodge, delivery was expected in Ogallala. The deal was not an unusual one, so Slocum kept his men and shortly the cows were delivered to Ogallala. The horses were not sold. At Ogallala the agent told him to have the cook and horse wrangler take the wagon and horses back to Texas, and that he would meet Slocum back in Dodge.

By this time, Slocum was getting itchy feet and wanted to move on. His men decided not to make the long, expensive rail trip back to Texas, but to return overland. Meanwhile, they were met at Dodge City by Ian McDonald, the man who had sold the cattle and hired them for the drive. There was one more job to do. It meant that Slocum as trail boss, along with one of the hands he selected, were to go to the collecting point at the nearby Indian agency and watch for the company's cattle that had been lost from all trail herds in the past. The cattlemen who held government beef contracts were expected to bring in some of the cattle lost from Slocum's drive.

And so each issue day Slocum and Tod Mulligan would recover some cattle from the various herds. The contractor would be permitted to sell the cattle as his own and he would then be allowed a few dollars for the trouble of gathering them. The balance of the money Slocum and his helper received in cash.

Slocum had no interest in returning to Texas. The drive had served its purpose for him, so he'd headed north, toward the Shoshone, Yellowstone, Powder River country, which he favored.

Finally, reaching the Greybull and the Absarokas, he felt something different enter him, while at the same time something else had let go. Now, with his eyes on the distant snowcapped mountains, he knew that he couldn't have said just why he was here, why he preferred this particular kind of life, in this country; he only knew that it was this that suited him. It had been a while since he had felt that way. Yet he knew, too, that real things didn't come with time. What was real was there all along.

"So they got the town sewed up tightern' a bull's ass in flytime," the old man was saying.

"Hunh," Slocum grunted, and poked at the small fire with the piece of branch he'd found for the purpose. "Vigilantes. Hunh!"

"That's what they call theirselves," Gulley added sardonically.

"You're sayin' the town was in such bad shape

the vigilantes were formed and took over to establish law and order." Slocum squinted across the fire at his companion.

"What I am sayin' is, that's what they bin claimin'."

It was dusk and they heard the sudden coughing of a coyote, not too far away. Both stopped, listening. And when it came again they both relaxed.

"It's a real one," Slocum said.

Something that sounded like a chuckle came from the mouth of his companion. "Hard to tell the difference 'tween a coyote and one of them Regulators," Gulley said. "They're wild, crazy like a pig with turpentine up his ass, and mean. I mean—mean!" He wagged his head to emphasize his words. "I seen one of 'em pick up a dog he didn't like who bin barkin' and botherin' him and throwed the poor sonofabitch right through a winder. You believe it!"

"How long has this been going on?" Slocum asked, studying the old man with extra interest.

"Since Borrocks come with his men and Miles Hammer let him take over."

"Who is Miles Hammer?"

"Sheriff. Got to be sheriff by electin' hisself over the dead body of the former sheriff, Tom Buckhorn."

"Buckhorn got himself shot, did he?"

"By Miles, by God. Neat as a whistle, wouldn't you say. 'Course I happened to see it. S'posed to make like a gunfight,'ceptin' Hammer braced Tom with his six-gun halfway already out of his holster."

"Mister Hammer likes a sure thing, it seems like," Slocum said dryly. "Is that how come the boys were after you?"

"Not directly that, on account of that was a while back and they knowed I wouldn't say anything. No, they likely have other reasons. Which I don't reckon it's necessary to go into, even if I knew," he added quickly.

"You mean, they'd got you by the shorthairs, but now they decided you're more dangerous than they figured."

Old Gulley's mouth pursed, then formed a grin and his blue eyes opened wide. "I allow that might be the God's honest truth for sure," he said, his words intoned like a preacher's.

"Doesn't seem to me you're a whole mite worried about it," Slocum observed, looking closely at the old man.

"Paw always told me and brother a man can't live forever."

"Except sometimes it's nice to make it a little longer than just right now," Slocum observed, keeping up with the laconic humor, and maybe even going one better, he reflected, as he watched Gulley's eyebrows shoot up and those bright old eyes blink in admiring surprise.

"By God, you got somethin' there, young feller. I do believe. Yessirree!"

"Let's cut the cackle, and get down to points," Slocum said, turning hard. "I want the straight of it."

"I kin only tell you what I know."

"The straight of it!"

The old boy waffled a bit at that, working his chew around his mouth pretty fast, like he was trying to fix it for spitting. Except he didn't spit, for suddenly, catching his companion's serious demeanor, which clearly meant no more nonsense, he blinked rapidly and swallowed a couple of times, his stringy throat emphasizing his Adam's apple as it pumped up and down.

"Like I said—like I bin tryin' to tell you, exceptin'

you keep interruptin' me—"

"I'm listening," Slocum said, and now his voice was hard.

The old man regarded the depth of the sky, but there was no support there.

"Like I said, Borrocks runs the Regulators, and Hammer first come out agin' 'em, saying his law-and-order bullshit, and how he's there to defend the people and all that malarkey. Only thing is, now it's clear as a whistle that Hammer's right in with Borrocks and his gang."

"I got'cha. Pretending to be against them, he can help them get away with it more easily."

"Somethin' like that," the old man said, sniffing and looking suspiciously at Slocum.

"Tell me about Borrocks."

"He's a hired gun, like the rest of 'em. But he claims the citizens is for him and his bunch."

" 'Course." Slocum nodded, his eyes on the fire.

"But now, the latest—Hammer give a speech just before my last run, night before, sayin' that he was now *for* the Regulators; that there was so much killin' and stealin' and like that, he needed their help, and he'd been maybe just a mite too suspicious of them at first on account of they ain't supposed to take the law in their own hands, but now he was deputizin' 'em so's to really clean up Bounty once and for all and make it safe, and all."

"I see. But—" Slocum let it hang, his cool green eyes fastening onto the other man.

"But what?" Old Gulley tried to look surprised, but Slocum could tell he knew very well what he was leading to.

Gulley was chewing fast now, as though that would help him collect his defense against the accusation he could see in Slocum's eyes and hear in his voice.

"But is there someone behind Hammer and Borrocks?" Slocum asked, his eyes directly on the old man, drilling him, "Or is it just the two of them?"

Gulley, realizing he'd dug himself into it, decided to just wait.

After a long moment, Slocum said, "They figured you suspected or maybe actually knew who was behind the whole setup, or anyway knew something about them; anyhow, enough to come after you, and pretty damn angry to boot." He had spoken right into the man hunkered near him, not allowing him an inch. And it was all guessing, built on what the old boy had said and implied.

But Gulley hung onto his silence.

After a while, Slocum added, "They won't give up. Plus, you can't go back to Bountyville."

"I'm headin' back," Gulley said. "I got to." And something in the old man's voice arrested Slocum so that he cut his eye fast right into the side of the other's face. Gulley was still staring at the fire.

"You have got to have a real good reason," Slocum said.

"I do." The words were spoken low and Slocum barely heard them, yet they were firm. He felt the old man's resolve.

"You going to tell me?"

Gulley was still staring into the fire.

"No."

"You sure?"

The old man turned to look at the man who had saved his life.

"Why'n hell should I tell you my personal business, Slocum, goddamn it!"

"First of all, that's just what you've been doing this past while. And second—" He didn't finish the sentence, but held his words, watching the other's reaction.

"Second what?"

"Second, which I'd put as first, you're protecting somebody."

"Slocum, I ain't—"

But Slocum was already on his feet, kicking the fire into its ashes. "That's your business, friend."

When they'd removed all sign of their camp, Slocum tightened the Appaloosa's cinch. Neither had spoken a word since Slocum had ended the conversation by standing up.

Gulley tried to make it aboard the Appaloosa without any help; in fact, this time Slocum hadn't offered any.

"Need a hand, by God," the old man muttered, his face dark with frustration after his third failure to mount the horse. "Dammit, you could hold his head, at least."

"So you do need a hand," Slocum said when Gulley was in the saddle. "That's what I've been telling you."

"To climb on this here animal with my game arm, sure."

"Listen; and listen good," Slocum said. "I am not in the Help-Bullheaded-People line of work. But I will likely be going through or maybe stopping over in Bountyville, and all I was interested in was the lay of the land. I can see you walking into big trouble and I'll be leaving you on your own just outside Bounty, if not sooner."

"You kin take off now, if you've a mind to," Gulley said.

"Shut up, and let's get out of here," Slocum said. "You ought to know by now it ain't good to hang around any one place for too long."

Slocum grabbed hold of the cantle with one hand and the saddle skirt with the other, and half-vaulted onto the Appaloosa, behind Gulley. It was a neat trick, but a tough one, and as before, he made it on the first try.

"Let's cut leather," he said. "Though keep him at a walk."

It was a good while later, with the sun just reaching the horizon, when either spoke.

"We'll make it soon now," Slocum said. "Town's up ahead."

The old man had been half-dozing, and now he shifted in the saddle.

"It's my daughter, Slocum. I'm afraid for her."

"That's a tough one then, for sure."

"I ain't sure they know her. But they got ways of findin' out things."

"That kind generally does," Slocum said, his voice dry as a bone.

"Thought I'd mention it; being as I owe you."

"You don't owe me anything," Slocum said calmly. "I'm just hanging in here for the ride."

Something that sounded almost like a laugh emerged from the man in front of him as the Appaloosa stepped briskly along, even under the added weight.

After another while, Slocum said, "Your daughter will be glad to see you then; she'll likely be hearing you caught lead by now."

Another moment passed and then Gulley said, "She don't know who I am. My daughter don't know me."

They fell silent as the evening came into the sky. Finally, Slocum said, "Well, good enough, then; that gives me two good reasons for hanging around Bountyville."

Old Gulley, sucking his gums and teeth alternately, allowed an even longer moment to pass, and then finally said, "How's that?"

Slocum's words fell casually into the slight chill that had entered with the night air. "Why, I hope to meet up with your daughter, I mean like a family friend," he added. "For one."

"And the other?"

"I'm looking real forward to meeting up with Mr. John Slocum."

Like a good many western towns, Bountyville looked as if it had been shot together. Casual. And yet, such towns were often magnets; for indeed, a town, as some sage had pointed out in one of the boisterous western newspapers, could be taken as a place to make your home and spend your life as part of a growing community. On the other hand, it could be a place where one escaped from life, from the world of names and history, where, in fact, a man could actually disappear. The great thing, Slocum had noticed about such communities, was that nobody asked your name or where you came from. To be sure, more often than not, nobody dared. The other great thing about such towns, as far as Slocum was concerned, was that anything—anything at all— could happen. And did.

Thus, seated in the Only Time Saloon, John Slocum, nursing a glass of flat beer, observed the girl who walked in and asked for a glass of water. She was extremely thin, her face was very white, almost pasty, and Slocum wondered idly if she had any breasts at all.

At the same time, he wondered about the man Old Gulley had told him about; the man who called himself John Slocum. Was he in Bountyville right now? Would he run into him? And how legitimate was he? Was his name really John Slocum? Gulley hadn't been able to help him much on that one, only repeating that the man existed, he'd heard of him, and he wasn't sure, but thought he had something to do with the Regulators.

"Ain't she a purty thing?" a voice suddenly said at his side. Looking up, Slocum regarded an ungainly young man with a big jaw, big hands, and a shock of red hair. His mouth was open. His lips were wet.

"I bet you some folks call you Red," he said, not able to think of anything else to say in the face of the surprising observation made by the young man, who must have been about twenty.

"Some folks do," his new companion said, sitting down at the table without asking, his eyes still on the figure at the bar, sipping her glass of water. "That is Miss Clementine Jones." His jaw hung open, and it was then that Slocum realized he wasn't quite all there. The slack jaw, the staring eyes, the fumbling hands, plus his general manner of a child who simply attached himself to another person—that is, his trusting behavior—caught Slocum up short.

"You know her?" he asked. "She a friend of yours?"

The young man—or overgrown boy, Slocum was thinking—turned away from the girl, but his eyes did not meet Slocum's. He was looking down at his hands.

"Red, you want somethin'?" The bartender called from behind the mahogany. But Red didn't appear to hear him.

"Can I buy you one?" Slocum said.

"Ain't she purty? I sure, boy, I sure—" And his lower lip began to tremble.

Slocum looked over at the man behind the bar, who

moved his head just slightly from side to side, and lifted his eyes.

Slocum had been leaning on the round table with his hands around his glass, but now he sat back, and at that moment, a big man from the small group at the far end of the bar detached himself from his companions and walked down the room to stand beside the girl with the glass of water. He leaned forward and, as far as Slocum could tell, he must have said something to the girl, for she suddenly drew back and threw her glass of water into his face.

Almost before the man recoiled in surprise, Red was up and across the short space and had slammed his fist into the big man's belly. But he had picked a tough one. The big masher didn't even budge, but simply seemed not even to notice the roundhouse right that Red had landed on him. Instead, he brought up his knee, driving it into the boy's crotch and, as Red doubled over, he rabbit-punched him to the floor.

But the fight was not over. Unnoticed, the bartender had reached for that faithful weapon known to everyone in the trade as a bung starter. This he laid on top of the bar in order to wipe his big hands dry to improve his grip. But the young lady who had been the center of the confrontation seized the bung starter and smashed it into the big bully's back, right across his kidneys. The man let out a great grunt of pain, but he was already being belabored about the head, the neck, his shoulders, and finally his kneecaps. Then, as he staggered and was about to fall, the small, thin, pale, and totally unhealthy looking lady drove that frightful weapon into his crotch. The bully fell writhing to the floor, where he lay groaning, his pain and anguish equaled only by the humiliation he was obviously undergoing.

Slocum, meanwhile, had not failed to notice the brace of six-guns the man was carrying, and was on the alert should he go for them. But the victim of the young lady's attack was beyond response. He could do no more than groan and clutch his crotch.

By now, the bartender had climbed over the bar and Red was up on his feet again. The girl—to Slocum's and everyone else's astonishment—had refilled her glass of water from a pitcher on the bar.

"Can I—uh—give you a hand, miss?" the bartender asked, not able to break out of his amazement with anything even nearly sensible to say.

"I don't need any," the lady said, putting down her glass. She walked over to Red, who was nursing his sore neck and, as far as Slocum could tell, looked utterly lost.

"Thank you, kind sir, for trying to help me. I am in your debt." The words were soft, yet firm, with the suggestion of a very faint English accent.

Red flushed all over his face and neck, right up into his flaming hair.

"Yes, m-m-m-m—" He stammered, as he stood in front of the wraith of a girl, fumbling with his hands, unable to know what to do with them.

"I am glad that the wild West has developed such heroic young men as yourself, sir."

Meanwhile, the bar crowd had gathered, and almost to a man were staring at this tableau as though thunder and lightning had just struck them all.

"My-my name—is H-Her—Lang-Langel-l—"

"Langley," the bartender said. "His name's Herbert Langley. Everybody calls him Red."

"And I am Clementine Jones," the girl said, speaking to Red.

"I-I know—"

"Then perhaps you can escort me to my home. I am feeling rather faint again, and the water didn't really help."

She offered a skinny arm, and the boy took it as though he was afraid of dropping it. Together they walked out of the saloon, while the crowd followed them with staring eyes, rooted to the spot, their mouths agape.

Slocum had remained seated throughout the altercation, and now he took a pull at his beer. The bartender returned his bung starter to its proper place, the drinkers returned to their places at the bar, and the victim of Miss Clementine Jones's onslaught got shakily to his feet and leaned on the bar for support. But he could find no man's eye in that collection of drinkers, and after downing a shot of whiskey, he decided to leave, throwing a furious glance in Slocum's direction as he limped away.

Five minutes later, the bartender, a fat man with a wen on his otherwise clean-shaven chin, approached.

"Mr. Clime wants to see you." He nodded toward the door. "He's got his office in that big stone house the end of the street."

Slocum lifted his head and regarded the fat man quietly. "Who?"

"Mr. Hoving Clime."

"Never heard of him."

The bartender's thick lips pursed at that. He took a breath and said, "Man runs this town."

"I can see he's doing a real good job."

The bartender, whose name was Cecil, seemed to hesitate. Slocum was watching him closely, and he wondered if the fat man was thinking of his bung starter.

"Mister, when Mr. Clime wants to see a man, the man best get hisself over."

Slocum said nothing. He had reached into his shirt pocket for a wooden lucifer and was now holding it in his mouth like a toothpick.

"Ain't my business, mister, but—"

Slocum looked up at the fat man then, squinting one eye. "You mean it damn well is your business on account of I don't get over there, he'll take it out of your hide. Right?"

Cecil said nothing. He stood there, his lips sealed, a single drop of perspiration slipping down the side of his bulbous red nose.

Slocum saw him throw a glance at the swinging doors then, and he said, "You can give a message to your friend out there on the boardwalk. Tell him to tell Mr. Clime I'll be settin' here for the time it takes me to finish my beer."

And he reached for his glass.

3

On the journey west the big man had studied the land, now and again stopping the wagons and climbing down from his Conestoga to squat there and crumble the soil between his thick fingers. He considered the height of the grass, seeing lumber in the great clumps of pine and strong timbers in the cottonwood and spruce that bordered the washes and creeks.

When he finally came to the place deep in the mountains called Last Chance, he found it nearly deserted, with only a few crumbling log cabins, sagging, washed-out log huts, dugouts, and two roofless stone houses.

The place, he discovered, was one of the earliest settlements in that part of the high country. An adventurous sect of religious whites had originally settled there and named it Lords Town. Devoted to God and the total subjugation of the native population, they had been wiped out by those heathen savages who they had tried so heroically to convert to the way of the Lord. Unfortunately, the uncivilized barbarians had not appreciated the means of such persuasive conversion:

27

the gun, the whip, chains, incarceration, prayer. The final result some years later was what greeted the eyes of that curious daring traveler, Hoving Clime.

At first glance, topping the lip of a long coulee, he had thought the place was a ghost town, deserted. He was greatly surprised to discover that it was, in fact, somewhat populated.

Something had attracted people to the devastated hamlet. There was a handful of survivors of the massacre who had escaped the Indians and had crept back to the broken hovels, somehow managing to start a new life for themselves. This had not been easy, so many had resorted to highway robbery. The pickings were lean. But there was another element—luck. For Last Chance was not a great many miles from the Canadian border and was considered a handy port of entry from either side to the other for those who found it necessary to escape the law. It soon became a haven for fugitives from Canada, and also for those who had good reason to disappear from the States. Only the most determined hand of the law would even consider trying to reach a person at such an address.

Somehow, in spite of the unholy trials and tribulations that this geographically unique hamlet had suffered since it had been founded, it had not only survived, but had, in fact, developed its own unique character. It was now, if not a fancy, first-class haven, then at least a port of call for the weary fugitive from the law.

At any rate, it was certain that Hoving Clime, a man of more than usual parts—a thinker, a doer, an adventurer in the old sense of the word—found something, saw possibilities in Last Chance that arrested his attention.

His cold gray eyes had surveyed the wretched hovels housing the few desperate people who had dared to return following the massacre. There was a saloon and a sort of inn combined, though it smelled so terrible that Clime refused to stay in it. Instead, he made his home in his wagon, while he pondered the strange reason why he was attracted to such a place. Yet he knew that this had to be it. Something—he couldn't name it, nor did he try—simply called to him. That was enough.

Awakening one night in his wagon, he sat bolt upright on his blankets and listened; listened to the voice of the Lord. He sat absolutely still, transfixed, enraptured, in a trancelike state that was all but suffocating, and that lasted he never knew how long. It could have been an hour, it could have been a second. It didn't matter. It was The Call. Then he knew why he was in Last Chance.

Twice before in his forty years he had heard The Call. Both times he had followed it—with profit. At the same time, it was not something he could have put into words, even to himself. It was simply something that happened, and he didn't question it.

Hoving Clime didn't waste a moment. The next day he started to fulfill his dream. A man of action, clear vision, and bold thought, he knew very well that in such a locale, with such shiftless people, one man with a purpose could do a lot. It took courage, vision, ingenuity, drive, and the ability to see—though not tarry over—more than one side of an argument. Clime now knew what he wanted, and he was going to get it. The Call had been just what he was waiting for: verification. Nothing more need be said. Armed with the great force of the creation, nothing could stand in his way. Out of chaos he would create order. Out of the wreckage of the cesspool of sin and iniquity that lay before him in Last Chance, he would create a community worthy of mankind and the Creator who had decreed the conquering of the wild West.

As the popular saying went, Clime did not let the grass grow under his feet. He moved into the larger of the two abandoned and roofless stone buildings, and with some of the younger members of his wagon train, began putting up a log roof. The rest of his party, some twenty-five persons, including his wife Marlene, a handsome woman older than Clime, began cleaning up the other buildings.

Not far from the town, a thick stand of spruce afforded long, straight building logs, at least eight inches in diameter. These were felled, then dragged along the ground by teams of horses, while thinner logs were also cut to form the roof of Clime's house.

Just two weeks after his arrival in Last Chance, Clime posted a large notice on a cottonwood tree in front of his stone house.

The announcement stated that Hoving Clime, Leader, was opening an office in his home and was ready for business. Any person of good repute who wished to engage in farming and ranching should apply to him. All persons who were already occupying land were to come forward at once to prove their right to do so. Those who were not able to produce legal title to their land would either sign up with Hoving Clime and take what land he would give them, or they would forfeit title. All others would get out.

Clime knew he held no official title to the land, but he had the members of his wagon train, some two dozen men and women, and in the course of rebuilding the town, he had acquired more followers. He had established the Sabbath, with services in the morning and again in the evening. All in all, he had been an agreeable addition to the broken town. When the citizens discussed the situation, no voice had been raised against the leader.

"The difference, you see," Clime was saying to the woman seated on the horsehair sofa across from him. "It is the difference that counts."

She was a young, dark woman in her early thirties. She wore a calico dress, her dark brown hair was tied back in a bun, and she had on spectacles, for she had suffered poor eyesight ever since childhood. Her name was Caligula, Callie for short.

"The difference?" Her eyebrows, which were darker than her head of hair and were thick and handsome, now lifted to question the use of the word. Callie was a schoolteacher. In fact, she was slated to start the school that Clime was building out of the ruins of the other stone house similar to the one he inhabited.

"Yes, my dear. It is the difference between thinking about something and actually doing it. The world is full of thinkers, or at least dreamers, but few doers."

"Like yourself, I'd say." A slight smile appeared at the corners of her generous mouth.

Clime felt the stirring inside him which of late was becoming more familiar, and more tantalizing.

"My dear Callie, we are trying to build a community that will be a credit to the Lord and to our great nation. And for that vast undertaking we need men—real men—and women, too." He allowed his gray eyes to move over her copious bust, watching its movement as she breathed, it seemed to him right now, a little more deeply. And he wondered—

"My dear, all I can say for the present is that things are moving along as I had planned. We shall have a building for your school within the month. What I need to know from you is how the people are."

"The people?"

"Yes. The citizens of Bountyville. For instance, how are they taking to the new name?"

"A lot of them just call it Bounty. But they seem to be all right about what's been happening. I know a lot of folks are glad the robberies and horse thieving have let off some."

Her eyes were a very dark brown; they seemed to Clime almost black. Like great pools. And just as unreadable. Still, he had a notion, and he continued to wonder—

"Well, I thank you for your time; I know how busy you are." She smiled appreciatively. "I just wanted to know how to plan ahead for the school, how long it would be till we could expect the new classroom."

"Soon," Clime said, standing up. "I'm afraid I have to see someone now, my dear. I wish to talk with you more—uh—about—uh—things. But—" His words trailed away as she rose and went to the door.

As she was reaching for the knob, there was a knock.

"Stand away from the door!" said Clime. His tone was sharp.

She threw a quick glance at him, but moved.

"You never know what might be coming through if you stand right in front like that," he said, his tone softer. "I am sorry if I frightened you."

"I am not frightened," she said. "And I shall heed your advice."

He had walked to the door as the knock came again.

"It's Hammer, Mr. Clime. I delivered your message."

Clime had now opened the door, and a wide-shouldered man with a sheriff's badge on his shirt, a six-gun at his hip, and a piece of pigging string in his left hand, stood there.

Clime stood squarely in front of the sheriff of Bountyville. His eyes dropped to the pigging string.

"Just showing one of the kids how to tie a roping knot. Couple of them be hanging around the sheriff's office," Hammer explained, his eyes taking in the presence of Callie Smith.

Clime said nothing as he stepped aside to allow the woman to leave the room, and then, without another look at the sheriff, he turned his back and strode to his desk, which faced the big window overlooking the street.

"I saw you coming, Hammer. Where is he?"

"He's at the Only Time."

Clime's big head lifted; he had been looking at some papers on his desk as the sheriff spoke to him.

"Oh?" He reached to the breast pocket of his black broadcloth coat and said, "I take it he's not coming, then."

"Right."

"He say anything?"

"He said he'd be there for as long as it took to finish his beer."

Miles Hammer watched the cold grin cut into Clime's face.

"But you gave him the message the way I worded it. Nothing extra," Clime said.

"Cecil told it to him. I had Cecil covered from the door, just in case."

Clime's forehead wrinkled in surprise. "I see you're careful of that man, Hammer."

"I am careful of that man. I've heard plenty about him, and I know none of it is singing. That man is no one to argue with."

Clime reached up and rubbed the side of his nose with his thumb knuckle. "And what about Borrocks's man? How does he feel about having the same name and likely the same reputation?"

"Borrocks's Slocum is also no man to mess with, if you want my thoughts on it. For me, I just wouldn't want to be in the middle."

"Which one is the real Slocum, Miles? They both have the same name, but have they got the same ability?"

Miles Hammer studied it. He was a man not without courage, but he was no fool. "You know, Hoving—" He paused, his lips moving as he worked them along with his thought. "You know Burrocks thought up the idea."

"Not quite, Miles. It was I who made the suggestion to Borrocks, thinking that with such a powerful name on our side it would throw some fear into the outlaw element. But then I heard from my old friend Ian McDonald in Dodge that the real John Slocum had just delivered three thousand head of Texas cattle and was heading in our direction." His grin was cold. "I said I could use a man like that."

Now, seeing how the sheriff's mouth had dropped open, Clime gave an abrupt laugh. "Thing is, Miles, thing is to always have two, three, maybe even a half-dozen games working at the same time. Never put all your money into one jackpot, my lad." And he began to chuckle, his eyes closed, a single tear appearing in the corner of each. "Now our old friend Lady Luck had doubled our bet. We've got two Slocums. His big cheeks shook now as he laughed outright.

"See, Miles, a man like Slocum—and it's why it amused me so when you gave me his message, for I could have predicted it—I say, a man like Slocum is worth ten of—" He paused, his pointed tongue running along his upper lip as he considered his choice of words. "—ten of just about anyone else." And then, with laughter still in his eyes, "Present company excluded, of course, Miles." His voice became heavy with gravity. "You know, Miles, I count on you—"

Miles Hammer nodded. "I know, Hoving. I know that."

Clime rose and started toward the door of his office, and the sheriff rose quickly, too, realizing that the meeting had ended. Clime had ways of showing a man where he stood.

"Keep your eye on him, on Slocum," Clime said, his hand on the doorknob.

"And the other?"

"But of course. Borrocks is watching his Slocum. Now, I want to be sure that he keeps using that name. Especially now that the real Slocum is at hand, right here in Bountyville."

"He used it Saturday when they braced the Leatherby stage. Like you know."

"Good. Just let it get around that John Slocum is holding up the stage, plus travelers, and doing a little horse stealing and cattle rustling." He grinned. "More sooner than later, Mr. John Slocum will be coming to visit me. Like after you arrest him."

Miles Hammer's face let go of all its wrinkles as it opened in astonishment. But the sheriff made a swift recovery. "Like they say, Hoving, there's more'n one way to skin a cat."

At the door, Hammer nodded, but Clime simply looked straight at the sheriff. "Just remember, Sheriff Hammer, that it's only here you call me Hoving."

"Have you ever let me forget it?"

"Because there's also more than one way to get yourself skinned, my lad. And we don't want that, do we."

Looking into those cold, steady, stone-colored eyes, Miles Hammer nodded, a very slight nod, but it said all that was necessary.

When Hammer had gone, Clime walked to his desk and sat down. Yes, he was thinking, there was indeed more than one way to skin a cat or catch a jaybird. Or—

When the knock came now, it was soft and could barely be heard. But he had been waiting for it. He was on his feet instantly, striding to the door, yet he had not lost his caution.

"Who is it?"

The answer came with a scratching on the other side of the door.

"I knew it was my pet kitten," he said as he opened the door and Callie walked in.

Slocum had thrown his duffel in better places than the Trail Inn, which was a more-or-less resurrected version of the filthy squalor that had been the inn when Hoving Clime had arrived in the town then known as Last Chance. The place had been swept, somewhat washed, and at least now there were no bugs and lice.

The room clerk was a young man with a pleasant face, something that Slocum had discovered wasn't overly common in Bounty. At least the young man wasn't surly, and as they discussed the weather and the rebuilding that was going on in town, the youth loosened a good bit.

Slocum had just come back down from his room and asked directions to the barber and bath. The young man was looking at him with a good bit of curiosity, something a man didn't do in that time and place. But like much of youth, the boy was brash.

"Mr. Slocum, I—uh—was just thinking it funny, but you got the same name as another feller. You a relative? Not that I'm trying to learn your business, sir, but I—"

"But you better learn something, son." Slocum cut him off fast. "Out here you never ask a man his name or where he's from, unless you got plenty of something to back up your question." Smiling, he added, "Where you from? Not from around this country, I'd say."

The boy flushed all over his face. He couldn't have been more than eighteen. "I come out with Mr. Clime and his wagon train. Me and my sister Ellie."

"I see." Slocum was leaning on the counter now, and he had taken out his tobacco and papers. "So where are you from? Back East. That right?" He loaded the thin paper with just the right amount of tobacco and rolled it, licked the length of the smoke, and twisted the end. It hung on his lower lip as he put away his makings and fished into his pocket for a lucifer. The boy watched every move with his eyes wide.

"Sure would like to learn how to do that, mister, but every time I try it, I make a mess. Guess I got to just keep practicing."

"That's the size of it," Slocum said agreeably, striking the lucifer on his thumbnail, one-handed. "Practice is the only thing that gets you anywhere. You just about out of school, are you?" And he bent his head to the flame.

"I helped on my granddad's farm back in Ohio. I'm handy, but I don't know cattle and sheep and stuff like that, and Mr. Clime said he could use me here in the hotel."

"Good enough then," Slocum said.

"I also don't know how to handle a gun much, though I did some shooting, hunting with my dad's Henry. Dad's dead," he added quickly.

He had bright blue eyes, freckles, and a shy grin. Slocum liked him right off.

"I was talking about not being much with a handgun, though," the boy went on. "My name's Terence Flanagan. My friends always called me Terry."

"What do you like to be called?"

"Doesn't matter." He gave a smile then. "It's the way sometimes people call you that counts, is how I figure," he said with sudden wisdom.

"You say you've got a sister? What is she doing?"

"Got a job helping after some children."

"I see," Slocum said, though he was wondering why they had come out all the way from Ohio. But he felt he had already gone against his own advice by asking so many personal questions. And he had done so not merely for answers to what he'd been asking, but to stir the young fellow into maybe giving away information about the situation in Bountyville.

Yet, Slocum found he wasn't through. He had one more question, and now was the moment. "Something I can't figure, Terence," he said easily, leaning on the desk.

"Where you get the best whiskey in town, Mr. Slocum?" The boy grinned with good will.

"I was wondering where you heard about this feller named Slocum. Is he in town here? Still here? You ever see him?"

"I heard about him one day in the diner. Mr. Borrocks and a couple of his men were in eating breakfast and it was right after the stage got shot up. The Ambleville stage it was. And a lot of money got taken and the driver, Tod Malone got shot up."

"You heard the name Slocum then?"

"That's the first time, actually. Mr. Borrocks was saying how he'd heard this man Slocum was on that job, and maybe running it."

"Who is Borrocks?"

"He's the head of the Regulators, the ones that's helping Sheriff Hammer; and I hear now how they've become deputies, the whole lot of them. On account of there's been so much horse stealing and robbery and shootings and all; Mr. Clime and the town council ordered that there be more lawmen about. And since then, things have been better."

"I see. But has anybody ever seen this feller Slocum?"

"I reckon somebody must of or they wouldn't have said he was at the robbery of the stage."

Slocum grinned to himself at that, at the boy's picking it up so neatly, and also he admired his directness.

The boy was looking at him in a strange way.

"That look mean you're wondering if I'm the same as the man who held up the stage?"

"Why, no. No!" And Terence flushed deeply. "No, sir," he said again. "Like I heard of you one time, if it's all right to say so, mister." And he ran his fingers through his thick head of brown hair, which was parted in the middle. "And, well, it is exciting to meet you, is what I mean to say."

"It's real nice meeting you, Terence," Slocum said. "Let's have a cup of coffee sometime."

"Sure enough." Terence nodded his head in agreement with that suggestion, and then suddenly he froze, staring at something or someone directly behind Slocum.

But John Slocum had already turned, having heard the slight sound of a footstep on the boardwalk outside and the stirring of air as the front door of the hotel opened.

He turned to face a medium-sized man wearing a tight black shirt and brown California pants. He was also wearing a brace of Navy Colts, slung low enough at his hips to inform anyone who cared to know what his line of business happened to be. This gentleman was followed, and immediately flanked by two others, both of whom were armed, one with a holstered handgun at his right hip, the other with a similar weapon at his left. John Slocum thought it made quite a tableau.

"Get out of here, Terence," he said over his shoulder as the trio spread out just enough to indicate the hostility of their presence in the lobby of the Trail Inn.

"Just stay where you are, son," snapped the man in the center, the one with the brace of pistols.

"Do what he says, Terence," Slocum said.

"Good hoss sense," said the man in black. There was a sneer twisting his lips, and his bronze eyes glistened.

"State your business," Slocum said.

The man in the black shirt allowed a beat to fall and then he said, "I hear you bin going around Bounty tellin' people your name is John Slocum."

"Looks to me like you hear pretty good," Slocum said. "So what's that to your business?"

"My name's John Slocum."

Slocum felt himself open up all through his body. It was just the way he wanted it to be. "No, it isn't."

"Are you callin' me a liar?"

"You heard what I said. I said your name isn't John Slocum."

"There is three of us, mister."

"No there isn't. There is one and a half. Each of you added up makes three halves; that's one and a half men."

"We can outgun you; make you real dead fast."

"Oh? Maybe so. But I wouldn't try to make you dead, mister. I wouldn't want to kill you. That would be too easy. What I'd do would be shoot both your kneecaps off, so's you'd never walk again. Now get out of here before I do just that." And his body almost imperceptibly straightened so that he appeared taller. It was a trick he'd used before with braggarts, a kind of emphasis to add muscle to his words.

He watched the hesitancy in the man's eyes. But he was holding his attention right at its most keen, while his entire inside was open and loose. He was free of thought, free of any tension that would interfere with his purpose. And he knew they could feel that. Then he flicked a glance at the landing above.

"By the time you pulled that trigger you'd be dead, Slocum."

And Slocum knew he had won. "Glad you remember my name," he said. "I don't want to hear you trashing it anymore. Remember that."

His words had not been loud, nor especially hard, yet there had been a penetrating power in them that was unassailable.

The man in black tried to look away, but couldn't. Then, without a word, he turned and walked out of the lobby of the Trail Inn, his two companions following.

Slocum waited another moment, then turned toward the boy, who looked as though he was about to faint.

"You all right, Terence? You look like you could handle a drink."

"I—I'm all right—now." He was shaking his head, his forehead was wet with perspiration. "Mr. Slocum, h-how—how did you know those men would back down like that? There was three of them."

Slocum seemed to think for a moment and then he said, "Well, at a time like that, there's not much choice. You can either bluff or get shot right away."

"So it was like—like b-bluffing. But I don't see how—like."

"I let them see me cut my eye to the upstairs."

"Hunh! You mean, like you had somebody covering you?"

"That's the size of it. They figured it was safer to believe me."

"But what if they hadn't?"

"Why, then we'd have had one helluva mess in this lobby."

It was then that they both heard someone clearing his throat, and Slocum caught the click of a metal as the familiar voice came down from the landing.

"By God, I was hopin' those sonsofbitches would of called ya, Slocum. I was just waitin' to blow 'em off at the pockets with this here goose gun."

Slocum burst out with a roar of laughter. "By God, Gulley, you were there all along!"

"Sure was. Now, I reckon we be even. Exceptin' it don't mean we got to part company."

"Sure don't want to, with somebody that sharp about, my friend."

"You mean, you didn't know he was up there?" cried the incredulous Terence.

"Sure didn't. But I'm glad he was."

"Then—did those men know?"

"I can't say."

The boy was staring at him with his mouth open, his eyes popping. "And—and you challenged them even so! Not knowing you were covered!"

"Well, son, it wasn't exactly the time to stand around picking my nose," Slocum said dryly.

"But you could have been shot. Shot dead!"

"Man can't live forever," Slocum said quietly.

As he came down the stairs, Gulley said, "Son, you got somethin' to learn. You're brother to that nice young lady I see with Thelma Dyson's young un's, so I know I can tell you somethin'. See, it's like a man who handles guns, he's got to know somethin'—I mean, somethin' special. He knows he is already dead, so he don't have to worry it. See what I mean—"

But looking at the boy, Slocum could see that he didn't.

4

In the soft sunlight of the fading day, Mr. Hoving Clime sat reading his much-handled copy of the Holy Bible. It was one of his special pastimes, or, he would actually have put it more rigorously; it was his discipline. He liked the word discipline, always pointing out to people that it was connected to *disciple*. Hoving Clime saw himself as a disciple. Not, of course, anywhere near the level of the Twelve, but a moral, intellectual, and surely conscientious descendant. And a practitioner of the creed.

Of course, he had failed. It was part of the course that had to be run. No one escaped the great failure that came daily. But one endured. One suffered and went on. Prayer answered all sin. Especially that of the flesh. He, alas, was one of its victims; along with thousands, millions of others. But with the difference that he suffered for his falling from the mark. He was certain that no one suffered more. But then, too, it had to be realized that the Devil was an adroit enemy, and one who wished to be a responsible disciple had to

45

know the enemy in all his guises.

Numb with devotion and guilt over his recent descent into the pleasures of the flesh, Hoving shut the book and sat gazing out the window of his office. He closed his eyes. In only a trice the Devil struck again and he found his mind's eye gazing into the adorable curves and undulations, the wondrous orifices, of Callie, his wholly abandoned and completely natural and amoral companion, of but a short while ago.

They had started at the door as she had entered his office, and his arms had swept around her, while one hand swiftly and dexterously locked the door. His erection, bursting against his trousers, drove between her already parted legs.

"My love." He had breathed the words into her adorable ear, while his hands slid to her buttocks, already undulating with his. And she, opening her mouth wide, received his tongue, their salivas mixing, as their breathing accelerated.

"Can't we lie down?" she gasped, and drove her tongue deeper into his mouth.

"I want you standing up," he said, pulling back so that he could unbutton her clothing.

In another couple of moments they were both completely naked, although she did have one stocking still only half off her leg. And then she was down on her knees, accepting his rigid organ into her mouth.

"God," he whispered. "Oh, my God!"

Callie mumbled something, her mouth full of her great pleasure.

He had his hands on her big, firm breasts, rubbing the hard nipples, squeezing all that joy that was filling his eager hands.

"I've got to lie down," she gasped, letting his penis free.

But he lifted her up from her knees and, bracing her against the door, parted her legs with his stiff member and entered her in triumph, while she squealed with delight.

In this way they stroked, as both of them felt the weakness overtaking their legs. Finally, she lifted both legs off the floor to wrap them around his waist, and with her arms around his neck he carried her, their organs still undulating in unison, to the sofa, where he laid her down and they finally, with the utmost attention to that marvelous passion and nothing more, stroked their way to the final, apocalyptic consummation, drenching each other with total delight.

They lay half on the horsehair sofa and half off, gasping, wet with perspiration and with come on their legs and bellies.

Hoving Clime thought that he had never, never realized such passion. He lay with his arms around her, reliving the joy of the great moment, a feeling of gratitude for the achievement the Almighty had apportioned him.

Later, alone in his office, he relived the scene, even his after-pleasure in the memory of it as they had lain, still entwined, on the sofa. Of course, he had no way of knowing that his companion, who had subsided slightly less quickly than he, was equally grateful for the moment. Nor did he know that lying there, she had suddenly found herself wondering whether Boltmann's, the dry goods store, had received the material she had ordered almost a month ago, and which they'd promised would be in any day now.

• • •

"They say that Borrocks was the only one of Plummer's gang what excaped." Old Gulley punctuated that statement with a squirt of tobacco juice that landed in the exact spot where the tawny cat had been dozing only a split second before. "By jingo!" And Gulley sat straight up on his backless chair, staring in amazement at the cat who was pacing well out of range and looking back at him. "Hell, Theodore, I never figgered to hit yeh. Sorry. I am plumb sorry about that."

Slocum was grinning at the old man's concern. They were in Gulley's soddy at the edge of town, having just come from a visit to Doc Laratunda, where the victim of the Regulators' bullets and near-lynching had been pronounced on the mend.

Slocum had asked to accompany the old shotgun guard, for he was eager to pick up as much gossip and chitchat as he possibly could. As an old-timer he'd once worked for down in Texas shortly after the war had told him, "It don't hurt to know it all."

Slocum agreed. Especially now, since he was beginning to realize there was a great deal more than met the eye regarding the stage attack and Gulley's near-lynching, not to overlook the sudden appearance in his life of a man named John Slocum and his brace of gunslingers, plus the general tone of Bountyville and the interesting invitation from the man named Hoving Clime, who apparently had everything sewed up—cattle, sheep, the town, the ranchers—for miles in every direction.

Gulley sniffed loudly, "Borrocks, they tell me, was the only one of the Innocents—what Plummer and the boys called theirselves—that Cap Williams missed on." He sniffed, belched, scratched his knee, and said,

"Cap got most of them, though. Ives and the rest. And especially Plummer hisself. 'Ceptin' I do believe they was more. Some that come with Borrocks."

"And you're saying that maybe Borrocks is running the same kind of game here in Bounty that Plummer was doing up in Virginia City and Bannack."

"That's the size of it, like I see it." Gulley was still regarding Theodore with puzzlement. "So why'n the dickens don't you come on back here and lie down in the sun?" He shook his head, now cocking it at Slocum. "Goddamn cat. You can't never figger 'em." Suddenly, he shifted in his chair, and stood up. "Bet he wants some milk, but I ain't got any." He looked over at Slocum. "You got another o' them cigars have you?"

"Sure do. And I'll join you." He reached into his shirt pocket. "Happen to be my last two."

"Theodore don't smoke," Gulley said dryly. He glared across the room at the lion-colored cat lying with his head on his paws, his eyes gazing drowsily at his surly benefactor, the owner of the soddy where they both now made their headquarters.

"Me an' Theodore been livin' together this good while," Gulley observed in his by-the-way tone of voice, which by now Slocum realized generally carried a deeper meaning than just the spoken words.

Slocum realized that even though Old Gulley was a true man of the frontier—tough, durable, and with a dry humor that could survive pain, hunger, and old age—he was saying more as he spoke about his feline companion than a whole page of words could have done. He was saying that he was lonely, though Slocum would have bet a stiff pile of chips that the old boy didn't know he was saying just that.

"What's all this I hear about that fellow using my name then?" Slocum leaned back, watching the ring of blue smoke he had just sent toward the roof of the soddy. "That part of anything, you figure, or is he playing his own hand there? Or is his real name John Slocum? Hell, I don't believe it."

"Easton?"

"That's his name?"

Gulley nodded, "It is, or was. He's got yourn' now. But I know him, know his type. He—I do believe—come down from Red Lodge country with Borrocks. He's a tough one, all right, even though you backwatered him." A chuckle shook him for a moment, with the result that he took in too much cigar smoke and fell into a coughing fit.

"Nice of you to side me there," Slocum said.

"I figgered you could of handled it yerself," Gulley said, "but I enjoyed it. Always get a lift out of waterin' down one of them smart slickers like himself there, and his two buddies."

They were silent then, and Slocum saw that the old man's eyes had closed. Then they popped open and stared out at Slocum like two small, very light blue skies.

"No, I do believe that Easton, he was or is interested in building hisself a reputation, maybe at your expense. On the other hand, Borrocks might be usin' him in his takin' over the town."

"Borrocks wants to take over Bounty, you're saying?"

"Borrocks and I'd say Miles Hammer along with him."

"What about Mr. Clime?"

"I got no idea what Clime wants. He sure favors preachin', I can tell you that; and you more'n likely already know that. But what he's after, I got no notion."

"Maybe I'll go visit him then."

Gulley's eyebrows shot up at that. "I would think he'd more'n likely come visit you, from what you tell me about refusin' his invitation. What I'm sayin', young feller, is that you are in deep water with that man. Clime is rich, Clime is powerful, and Clime has something on his mind. Maybe he wants to get to be president or something like that. I dunno. But looks to me like he wanted you; and I don't believe him to be the kind of man gives up with only one try."

"I don't believe so either," Slocum said.

"So why don't you wait then? Not that it's any of my business."

Slocum stood up and took another drag on his cigar. "I'll turn it over," he said. "Meanwhile, I'm going to check out a couple of places. Might run into something; you never know."

Gulley sat up suddenly. He seemed more alert as he removed the cigar from his mouth and looked keenly at the man who had saved him from a particularly cruel form of hanging.

"You got to be careful, Slocum. That Easton, he's not gonna take what you handed him just like that."

"That I know."

"And we both got the feeling Clime wants you for something. Now, whether that's connected or not with Easton wantin' to backwater you or just plain shoot you, I dunno."

"Neither do I. But I'll be interested to let you know." And Slocum's grin was warm as he looked at the old man sitting in the old chair in his old soddy. Then he looked at Theodore. "Your daughter live in Bounty?"

Gulley looked away for a moment, then back at Slocum. "She does. Her name is Annie. Annie Gilchrist. That's her mother's name. Was."

"Where's her mother now?"

"Dead."

"Why doesn't your daughter Annie know you then? If it isn't my business, just say so."

"On account of her mother and me wasn't married. And it just happened by crazy accident that Annie's turned up here in Bounty. She was lookin' for her mother, I bin told. And she must've found out she—Alice—died of the croup this good while back. And I had sent Annie East, through a priest who knew some couple would take her. I wrote 'em Alice's husband was dead and I was helpin' out; a friend." He stopped suddenly. "Shit, here I bin runnin' my mouth again."

"But then why would Borrocks and them want to do anything to Annie? To get at you, right?"

Gulley nodded. He was chewing more slowly now. "That's the size of it."

"And you think they don't know about Annie, but then you're afraid they might somehow find out she's your daughter. That it?"

Gulley nodded.

"Somebody when I was in the place where she was workin' mentioned we looked alike. It got me to thinkin'. And worryin'."

"It appears, though, that Borrocks and his boys think you know something about them, maybe from the past."

"But by God, for the life of me, I got no notion what the hell that could be. I only know what I told you, but a lot of people know that."

Slocum was staring at him.

"You look like you don't believe me."

"No, It's not that. I believe you. They're afraid of something they think you know, and that you might tell somebody."

"But what?"

"Well, maybe we can try to find out." Slocum said. "That's why they made like they were going to lynch you, scaring you so you'd do what they wanted. That rope had too much play in it for a real necktie party."

"That's how it 'pears."

"Did they say anything to you when they were stringing you up?"

"Only that by God now I wouldn't be talking anything to anybody."

"But now they'll know you're back."

"And they'll try again, and maybe this time—"

"Where can I find your daughter?"

Suddenly, the old man was up and out of his chair. "No! You can't talk to her. See, now she knows her mother is dead, and has found out all she can about it, she'll go back East."

"Maybe."

Gulley was standing there, looking down at a spot on the earth floor of his soddy.

"They might have seen you and me talking together," Slocum said. "I'll be careful leaving here."

"What you think, Slocum? How you figure it?" Gulley now asked, after the brief silence that had fallen upon them.

"I think you'd better talk to your daughter."

"What good will that do? If anybody saw me, you know what would happen."

"Is there anybody here who knows about you and her mother?"

"I don't believe so, but I can't be sure."

"Nobody said anything about it when they were fixing to string you up?"

"Not a word."

"That's a good sign then. At such a time somebody would more than likely have a shot at that."

"I know what you mean. Nope, no one said a thing." Gulley was nodding his head.

Slocum had started to the door. The roof was especially low near the door of the soddy and he had to stoop a little. Gulley's next words stopped him right where he was.

"I trust you, Slocum. By God, you saved my life. But don't tell her who I am. She believes I'm dead. But I do believe if they find out they can get to me through her, then they sure as hell will."

"Then I need to know where to find her. And I need to know whether you know something about them that they don't want known or if it's just to set you up as an example to frighten the others into line."

"Hyaah! Hy-yaah!" The long whip cracked over the sweating team as the horses lunged, racing into the canyon, braces creaking and the coach teetering from side to side. Dust billowed behind the racing wheels, the iron tires ringing wildly on the rocky road.

The driver rode grim-faced, his hands tight on the leather lines, shoulders hunched, his feet spread on the box in order to give him purchase against the rioting movement of the racing stagecoach.

He was a bullet-headed man wearing a dusty black Stetson hat, with knobby shoulders, big-knuckled hands, and a scar running down the left side of his face. His orders were clear. The ambush lay just ahead, about half-way into the canyon. He knew exactly what to do.

Behind him in the coach rode four passengers, carrying between them a hefty amount of gold which they had taken from Virginia City after the demise of the Henry Plummer gang.

Yet, while Plummer was dead and his gang dispersed or hanged along with their leader, no one in the coach was riding easy in the knowledge that now the road was safe. For the Plummer tentacles had a wide reach. What was more, there was the rumor that some of the famous gang were still at large and plying their trade. Up on the box, Skinhead Hatcher was well aware that his passengers were concerned over possible trouble.

Beside him, Ty LaPlace checked his weapons, as he had been doing from time to time ever since the beginning of the run.

Inside the coach, the passengers were also heavily armed. Anticipating trouble, some carried shotguns, some rifles, and nearly all carried pistols as well. Skinhead had heard them saying that they were too well-armed to be attacked. That was back at the stage depot, and they must have had no reason to think differently right now. Plus, there was Ty LaPlace riding shotgun up there next to him.

Now, immediately ahead, the road made a sharp bend between two smooth slabs of rock. Skinhead slowed the coach to make the turn, pulling back hard on the leather lines.

Right then he saw the men in the road signaling him to stop. And he saw those partly concealed in the rocks on either side, too. He pulled harder on the reins as LaPlace shouted, lifting his gun, and received a bullet between the eyes, somehow managing to rise halfway to his feet, he then crumpled and fell like a sack of clothes to the dusty road.

From inside the coach, the passengers opened fire. Skinhead's whip cracked out. The team lunged ahead, then stopped abruptly as he hauled furiously on the lines. The passengers piled wildly into each other inside the coach, their aim spoiled.

None of the bandits wore masks, as indeed one of the cooler passengers noted, and he noted, too, that this was surely an ugly sign. One passenger, attempting to resist by raising his pistol, was shot through the window. Then both doors of the coach were pulled open and everyone was ordered to alight.

For appearances' sake, Skinhead Hatcher took his place with them, his hands in the air. He waited, his arms gradually lowering as he heard the shots racketing on the canyon floor. Then there was silence, the only covering that those corpses were going to have.

"Skin, give us a hand," one of the men shouted, as he strode forward, holstering his big Colt. "Where's it all hid?"

"Most of it's in the strongbox under the seat," Skinhead said. " 'Ceptin' that one there's got it sewed in a canvas money belt 'round his waist. And that one yonder's got something hanging 'round his neck, like a pouch."

A half-dozen men had pulled it off, and as they rode away, they knew it had been worth it. Briskly, they thundered up the long, low canyon slope and topped the ridge, leaving a thin trail of dust behind them. Skinhead Hatcher, whose role had been to drive the team to the next stage stop and report the ambush, thought better of it as he viewed the massacre, and decided to ride with his buddies.

Back down on the floor of the canyon, the coach horses fussed, turning their heads, then shaking them as a shift in the coming night wind carried the smell of blood to their nostrils. All at once, alarm at the smell of death touched them and they lunged ahead to get away from the grim odor. But they had no driver, and, running too close to the edge of the road, the coach tipped, dragging the terrified horses down in a maelstrom of flying hooves and tangled harness.

By the time the six men and Skinhead Hatcher reached their destination, night had long since fallen, but their companions were waiting for them. Around a blazing fire in one of the most remote box canyons some miles from Bountyville, at least two dozen men gathered with their leader as the loot was dumped onto a blanket spread on the ground.

Somebody produced scales and a good two hours were spent in weighing and dividing what had been taken from the stage passengers.

It was, of course, Borrocks who reaped the lion's share, even though he had not joined the action but had given over the actual charge to a lesser man. It was always thus, and it had never been questioned— the right of the leader.

"It was a good one," somebody said as all stood happily watching the blanket being folded. A bottle had been produced, then another, and the men were reaping the pleasures of reward and the envy and congratulations of their fellows who had remained in camp.

"That it was," said someone in response to the first speaker, only to find himself flat on his back as the result of a blow in the neck from Borrocks.

"You stupid shits! What the hell d'you mean, patting yerselves all over like you done somethin' special. If it hadn't been planned right you'd all be down there with the dead ones, by God! Don't you never let me hear a one of you congratulatin' yerselves like that. You're a bunch of greeners, fer Christ sakes! You're still wet back of the ears! And you!" He spun on Skinhead, his fury roaring out of him like a wall of fire.

Skinhead was a brave man, but he blanched under the attack. The next thing he knew he was flat on his back, having received a fist that felt like the hammer of a blacksmith along the side of his head.

Borrocks stood over him, spread-legged. "You goddamn ass! You fool! You were supposed to bring the stage back into the depot and report what happened. Now they'll know you were in on it, and they could just as lief get smart to our setup on who's carrying what on the stages. You goddamn shithead!" And his boot drove into Skinhead's ribs—once, twice, three, four times—while the wretched victim tried to roll away, screaming in the rising dust until one blow of his leader's boot cracked him in the spine and his scream cut through the night sky like a scarlet knife. And then he was silent.

"Is he dead?" somebody asked.

Borrocks's big head swung around. "Who the hell wants to know!"

Nobody answered.

From somewhere high at the top of the canyon wall came the howl of a coyote.

To John Slocum, it came like a wind, only stirring at first, but rapidly gaining force as it swept through the town to announce itself as the chief presence in Bountyville, while wagging tongues eagerly awaited a name or names on which to hang the outrage of the holdup and murder of the four travelers and the shotgun rider on the Bountyville-Four Buttes run.

He heard it in the saloons, the coffee house, the Trail Inn, in the stores, in the street. Yet, it was muted, for who could be sure? Who could be sure that he wouldn't quite by error find himself on the wrong side of the creek? And so, while the anger was there, it was expressed in ways that often the one expressing it was not aware of.

Slocum had heard it first from an excited Terence at the Trail Inn. His eyes were huge, his mouth wide, and his breath not wholly free, as he announced the grim event.

"But it's happened before," Slocum said.

"Sure. Lots of times. But not so open-like." The young man ran his fingers through his thick brown hair. "I dunno. It—it seems different. All that killing! It's—It's scary." He paused, rubbing the palms of his hands together. "Kind of," he added, as though fearful of giving away some of his hard-earned manhood.

"You've got a notion, have you?" Slocum asked. He was leaning on the desk in the lobby. No one was about; it was the middle of the afternoon. Yet, while the lobby of the hotel was all but empty, it still felt to Slocum as though there was a kind of tremor in the air. He felt it and he believed in it. Bountyville and its inhabitants were on the edge of something. He wanted to locate Annie Gilchrist. Gulley had told him that his daughter lived with a Mrs. O'Brien and had worked at the Yellowstone Clothing Emporium, but had recently left to take another job. Since he'd been away, he wasn't sure just where she was now. And Slocum didn't want to go to Mrs. O'Brien's to ask for the girl directly, anyway. With Terence he was quite roundabout.

"Reminds me of the time a friend of mine back in Dodge got in the middle of a gun argument between the Mastersons and a gang known as the Lighters. My friend was named Gilchrist. Matter of fact, he might have come out to these parts, I mean the Powder River country. You happen to know any Gilchrist around?"

His game worked, for the boy was already nodding. "Sure do. There's Miss Annie Gilchrist at the Yellowstone Clothing. But she don't sound like your friend who got mixed up with the Mastersons and that other feller." He grinned.

Slocum was serious now. "You reckon the Regulators are going to start looking into this holdup doings?"

"I'd guess so. That's what we've been told they were hired for, to be acting deputies. I know folks have had enough of all the robberies and holdups and shootings and the like. Exceptin'—"

"Excepting what?" Slocum asked, stepping back from the desk as though getting ready to leave.

"Nothing."

"Excepting the Regulators pump as much lead and sometimes more than the ones they're supposed to be bringing to justice. That it?"

The young man was nodding. "That's it."

"I'll be back later," Slocum said. He had just started toward the front door, when through one of the side windows he saw the men coming down the street.

"There a back way out?"

Terence pointed, seeing the three men himself now. "I'll talk to them," he said, and he was happy to discover that his voice was steady.

But John Slocum was already gone. There was no point in hanging around when a thunderstorm was gathering. And he had a strong feeling those men

were looking for him. It figured. It would fit the
puzzle he'd been trying to piece together regarding
Hoving Clime.

He had considered asking at Mrs. O'Brien's or at the
Yellowstone Clothing Emporium, but decided against
it, not wanting to attract attention to himself or the girl.
He did walk into the Yellowstone, however, to see if
he could spot anyone that might fit the picture he had;
even though she had ceased to work there, there was
a chance she might have stopped by. Even more than
that, Slocum often worked on intuition, and understood
that sometimes going to a place where a person had
been might just possibly furnish something in the way
of a clue.

But there was nothing forthcoming. The store was
almost empty, with no one even within the girl's age
bracket. He pretended to be looking for someone, then
left, deciding on a much needed cup of coffee.

At the Happy Times Eats he ordered a cup of coffee
from the young waitress and then added, "And a steak
and spuds, along with it." He was glad to find the place
empty.

"Very good." And she smiled.

No, he decided, she didn't look like Gulley in any
way at all. That is, not until she turned and he saw
her back. Her hair was done up on top of her head,
and he caught the nape of her neck. It was then he
knew her. And when she returned with his coffee, he
was sure of it.

For some strange reason, he had thought of her as
being much younger. And yet, thinking on it now, he
couldn't figure why. She looked to be in her middle
twenties, but what struck him most forcefully was not

her good looks so much as her movement, her voice, the open, clear way she looked at him. She was quite obviously a person unafraid, the way so many people were in their almost-hidden ways. Annie Gilchrist was as open as a child. Plus, she had a delightful smile and a superb figure. She moved through the atmosphere around her as though she owned it. As far as Slocum was concerned, she did own it. Yet there wasn't a shred of arrogance in her. She owned her place as a small child would own it.

But it was her eyes that totally claimed him. They were large and brown, and he had only really seen such eyes in small children and animals.

She had brought the milk pitcher. "The steak will be along. And I'm bringing baking powder biscuits. They're just fresh."

"You can read minds," he said.

"I can read when someone is hungry and needs solid food," she answered. "Now, if that coffee seems a bit old, leave it. I've already put on a fresh pot."

"I do appreciate it, miss."

"Is there anything else you need, sir?"

"I need to know your name."

"I see." She gave a little laugh, and then started off. "I believe the coffee's about to boil over."

He liked the way she'd handled it. Yet, while he didn't want to start out with her on the basis of simple physical attraction, it was quite obvious that it had taken that turn with his opening sentence. Somehow, he felt the need to keep everything on a simple businesslike basis. And the point was underlined when she brought the rest of his order, smiled very pleasantly, but made it quite clear that she was not interested in him as a male possibility.

On the other hand, how could he get to know her without her feeling that and that alone was his purpose? He certainly couldn't mention Gulley. Then, what could he bring up as a subject for conversation?

At that point he suddenly broke out into a laugh, telling himself that he was getting a little loco and old before his time. What was the matter with him making a big hassle about a pretty young girl? Except, not pretty; she was much more than pretty.

"Are you talking to yourself, mister, or have I missed something?"

Her words fell on him like birdsong and now he roared with a huge laugh at himself, realizing how the tension that had been building in the town had gotten into him and because of the radiance, the sweetness, and at the same time the unbelievable innocent sexuality of the girl, he'd been thrown. It just went to show that the devious approach to important matters was always a terrible mistake.

She was staring at him in mild surprise, having just brought his food. He thought she had the softest brown hair he'd ever seen, the brownest eyes, and the lobes of her ears, which were barely visible, assured him that every other particle of her had to be in keeping—the unseen along with the seen.

"Would you be wanting some water?" she asked.

"I was just thinking something."

"What? Or maybe I shouldn't ask."

"That your voice is as good-looking as the rest of you."

"I have a terrible temper," she said, quite matter-of-factly.

"I'm very glad to hear that," Slocum said. "I was afraid for a moment that you didn't."

At that they both laughed.

"I have to get back to the kitchen," she said suddenly. "Something's boiling over. I hope not—" She didn't finish. She was already running.

The door opened and two men walked in. The atmosphere in the small room instantly turned cold.

"Mister Clime wants to see you, Slocum."

They had spread out; both were wearing handguns, slung low. There was no question that they were not going to accept another no. But John Slocum was a man who had always carried an excellent sense of humor.

"Well now, I sure don't want you two fellows to lose your forty-and-found on my account." He grinned at them, nodding to a couple of chairs. "Pull up those two chairs and you can have some coffee while I get outside this fine looking steak."

"Cut it, Slocum, and let's get moving."

It was the one to his left who had spoken.

"Carl—" His companion nodded his head. "We'll take him up on his offer. We've got the time."

"Shut up."

Out of the side of his eye Slocum saw the girl start to enter the room from the kitchen.

"Stay out of here, miss," he said, as both the men turned to look at her.

And in that instant of inattention he had shoved the table at them, drawn, and they were covered.

The room was silent as a stone, save for the drip of coffee from the overturned cup as it ran onto the seat of the chair next to Slocum.

"You fellers drop your guns. And then you turn around and get out of here."

He watched the bigger one shooting his eyes from side to side. His companion's lower lip began to twitch.

"Boys, I said unbuckle!"

The gun belts, along with their contents, dropped to the floor. As one of the men stepped back, at Slocum's signaling him to do so, he knocked over a chair.

"Pick that chair up before you take off," Slocum ordered. "And that table setting there on that one, you straighten that real neat now."

They did so.

"Now git. And tell Mr. Clime to listen better next time when I send a message. I'll be here finishing my dinner, and then, well, we'll just have to see."

When they had gone, he apologized to the girl. "I had no notion those fellows were still wanting me," he said. "And I'm sorry they disturbed you."

"Oh, it was my pleasure," she said with a wry smile. "I find life pretty dull and uneventful in Bountyville and it's bracing to have entertainment brought right into one's life."

"You talk like you've been to college," Slocum said, grinning at her sense of humor.

"Back East where life is also exciting, but nowhere near so often as out here where all the interesting people seem to gather."

And then they were both laughing again.

"My name is John Slocum," he said.

"I figured that when the gentlemen on the left made the introductions," she said with a small smile, her tone dry, and her eyes looking at his Stetson hat.

Without a word, he reached up and removed it and laid it on the chair beside him.

"What did you do that for?" she asked.

"My maw always tried to teach me good manners. She always said you were never to wear your hat or gloves while eating. I remember the glove part but I always forget about the hat."

"I reckon you're not a real westerner then, Mr. Slocum. A western man's always naked without his hat."

"Well, if you can stand it, I can."

A tiny smile teased the corners of her mouth. "My name's Annie Gilchrist," she said.

5

Slocum had argued with the old man to move out of his soddy, at least, but he found he was arguing with the wind.

"I ain't lettin' them reptiles scare me outta my house, by God! And I got my goose gun waitin' for 'em when they comes by."

"That the only weapon you've got?" Slocum had asked him.

"It's all I need. Had two, but you seen what happened to the other at the holdup."

"I heard the company wants you to move down to Lander. I hope they're helping you."

"I'm stayin' here. Those mealy-assed sonsofbitches ain't scarin' yours truly outta his house and home!"

Together they let their eyes wander through the room that was the old man's house and home—the dirt floor, dirt roof, dirt walls built into the bank that ran along part of Holy Creek on the south side of town. Not so long ago wolfers had made it their headquarters.

Slocum said nothing after his eyes covered the space that Gulley called home. He had thought to tell the old man about meeting his daughter, but decided against it. And anyway, it would serve no purpose that he could see at the moment.

"You don't seem too worried about them trying again," Slocum said after the silence had grown heavy.

"They know I don't know anything important about them. They was just tryin' to scare others from knowin' anything. Hell, a man can't live longern' his time anyways; no matter how hard he tries."

"You can come stay in my room at the Trail Inn if you've a mind to," Slocum said.

" 'Preciate it."

And that had ended the conversation. Following that episode, Slocum had returned to the Trail Inn, talked a minute or two with Terence at his desk, learned that nobody had been looking for him, and then had told the boy that he would be heading out of town.

"Want anyone to know that?" Terence had asked.

"Sure do," Slocum said. "I'll be gone two, three days. Maybe more. But you don't know where. And you don't know when I'll be back."

"I understand." Terence's young face was grave. "I feel something is building up, Mr. Slocum. Do you feel that?"

"It often feels like that in some of these faraway towns. Something builds up and up and then either peters out or explodes, and then everybody goes back about his business again. And you start over."

"I see."

"You worried?"

"I don't want anything to happen here in the hotel."

"You had enough excitement, did you, when those three braced me?"

Terence nodded vigorously. "I—I was wondering if you could give me some teaching on how to handle a gun, Mr. Slocum. Would you have time? I couldn't pay you very much, but anything you could do to show me something would be a big help."

"It's better to stay away from the guns, Terence, except you want to shoot some game; like that." He grinned at the young man, liking him, and hit his fist lightly on his shoulder. "I'll show you a couple of things maybe when I get back. I say maybe. But I don't want you to get the notion that you're going to be a gunfighter or something. Remember that the only smart gunfighter is the dead one."

"Dead! What do you mean by that? The only smart gunfighter is the dead one? That's like Mr. Gulley said that time."

"Because when a man accepts he's already dead, he's got nothing to lose. That makes him free. He's not afraid, and he can do anything."

Down at the livery, giving the Appaloosa a good brushing, he wondered why he stuck around. He had only come here because of Gulley, and he had only stayed out of a sort of mild curiosity. Now, of course, there was the girl; and that was something surely pleasant to think about. But did he need to mess around with Clime, whoever he was? And Borrocks? Noah Borrocks: The full name came to him suddenly and he realized he had heard it, knew something about it, from somewhere. Where? The war maybe?

He had never heard of Hoving Clime before. But he'd heard plenty since he'd come to Bountyville. Clime was big, Clime was rich, Clime was a doer; the kind who were always talking about building the West; but they were also the kind that often actually did a lot of building. Was Clime connected with Borrocks, the self-named vigilante who was raising such hell in this part of the country? And then, why had Clime wanted to see him? And what was this business with a man named John Slocum?

He wondered as he put away the brush and the old shirt he'd been rubbing the Appaloosa with if maybe that was why he'd been sticking around Bounty: curiosity.

No, he didn't think so. And yet, somehow, though he was sure he had never heard the name Hoving Clime before, he felt he had known something; that is, there was a certain familiarity, something had rung a bell in him, and did it again whenever he thought of Clime or heard something about him. It was—and he felt certain of this strange thought—it was that, while he very likely had never laid eyes on Clime, didn't know anything about him or his activities as such, he was somehow familiar with his way, his method. Yes, it was that. He knew now that he had either heard of the man before he came to Bounty, or had heard something of him, though not by name, somewhere, some time. Suddenly the thought struck him like a hammer.

Did Clime want to meet him, confront him, because he knew something about him? Something that was more than just the John Slocum reputation?

And now another thing struck him. Was the fake John Slocum—the man whose real name was Easton—was he in fact a kind of decoy to attract him?

He stood beside the Appaloosa in his stall, half aware of the cruising deerflies, the smell of horse manure and leather, and the slight ticking of the hay above him in the loft—and he wondered.

• • •

Thanks to the fact that he decided to check the shoe on the Appaloosa's left forefoot, his departure had been delayed. He had planned to scout the area around Medicine Creek, the country that was riddled with box canyons, furnishing a veritable maze of rock defying the most able tracker or determined lawman to penetrate it.

The shoe was loose enough to require being pulled, and Slocum spent the best part of an hour putting on a new one. While he reshod the Appaloosa, he had a chance to chat with Harold, the hostler. It was mostly gossip, but it fleshed out some of the facts he'd caught from Gulley and things he'd heard about town.

The Appaloosa had been easy enough to handle until, kicking at a deerfly that buzzed his crotch, he upset Slocum's balance, for he'd been holding the horse's foreleg between his own two legs as he clipped off the end of the nail protruding from the wall of the horse's hoof. The result was that Slocum almost fell, but managed to right himself. His recovery was aided by a few choice words blistering the air as he aimed them at the deerflies who seemed to delight in their game. But then, like a clap from above, a light, airy young voice reconciled the whole scene of battle between man and deerfly.

"Excuse me, sir, but can you tell me where the liveryman is, or is it—you!" The final word came out in surprise as Slocum raised up to face the very person he'd only just been thinking about.

"No, I'm not the hostler, but if that's who you're looking for, then I wish I was."

She smiled at that. He had let go of the Appaloosa's foot and had straightened up.

"I don't want to interrupt your work, but perhaps you could tell me where the liveryman, or hostler as you called him, happens to be."

"He was here and said he was going for a cup of coffee. Maybe he went to your place; but then maybe you aren't working today. Can I help you?"

"I wanted to hire a saddle horse."

"Well, I can show you what's here, and maybe help you pick one out, and by then Harold might be back."

"I don't want to interrupt your work, Mr. Slocum—"

"It is my pleasure, Miss Gilchrist."

He walked slowly toward the open door leading into the livery and she fell in beside him.

"Have you ridden much?"

"Some. I don't want any wild bronco, but on the other hand, I don't care for a horse that is too slow."

"That little pinto pony down there in the corner looks to me like just the one for you," Slocum said.

"That there 'little pinto pony' as you calls him just happens to bee-long to Mr. Hoving Clime and is not part of this here hiring establishment. That hoss is a boarder, like yourn', mister, that App-loosa."

"Ah, here's Harold now," Slocum said with a big grin at the testy old man's sudden appearance from out of the shadows of the big barn.

"Enjoy your coffee, Harold?"

"Tasted like it'd spent the overnight soaking in barbwire to toughen it," snapped the old man, his jaws bulging as he clamped down on his words. "I believe you might favor this little blue roan, miss," he said now, and Slocum took note of how his tone softened for the girl. The old buzzard wasn't so old after all, by golly!

"And I'll need a saddle."

" 'Course. Wasn't figurin' on you ridin' him bare-back." He glared at her, though without hostility. "You riding both sides or the one?" His eyes had dropped to take in her riding britches.

"Both sides."

Then, to Slocum's utter astonishment, the girl had turned toward him and with a hint of a smile had said quite simply that as it was her day off from work, and since the weather was so beautiful, she and her friend had decided on a picnic together. At the last minute, her friend couldn't come and here she was with a picnic basket for two. Would he care to join her? She was not going to spend too much time, but enough to enjoy the lovely day.

"I knew there was a real important reason why I hammered a new shoe on the Appaloosa," Slocum replied.

Later, sitting by a creek, Slocum was not surprised to find that she had made a delicious picnic. He could see that she was a person who knew how to do things well. At the same time, it had to be admitted that her fine character traits were outweighed by her beauty.

Slocum, desiring her as much as he did, still felt no need to hurry. He realized that she felt the same, and that both of them were simply obeying an ancient law of attraction leading to resolution, or completion. And so it was not necessary to do anything. It was simply happening; allowing it to happen was one of the best things about it.

The sun was warm on them as they finished their lunch by the little creek. It was just past noon, the sunlight was dazzling the water, and a light, occasional breeze stirred the box elders and whispered over the lush grass at the bank of the creek.

They had been silent for a moment, and now, as the moment lengthened, Slocum felt something inside him reaching out. But he stayed where he was without moving. Then all at once—and it seemed that neither one of them had made a move—they were looking at each other, looking and falling into the other's eyes.

They had already spread a blanket for their picnic and now he slipped his arms around her, and kissed her on the mouth. Her lips were soft, yet completely answering his, as her arms circled his neck, drawing him down as she lay back, her legs parting to receive the thrust of his bold erection.

Without hurrying, he undressed her, starting at the top to remove her blouse so that her creamy breasts with their hard, erect, dark nipples were free; bowing his head, he took one nipple in his mouth while fondling the other breast with his hand.

Meanwhile, she was opening his trousers and now, grasping his hard organ, pulled it out and placed it between her legs. But she still had her underpants on, and these he deftly removed. In another moment they were both stripped, lying naked under the hot sun, as he sucked her breasts, taking turns from one to the other, and she stroked his member, which was just about bursting, and played with his balls.

"I want you—" Her words breathed into his ear, and her legs spread as she lifted her knees and guided his cock into her thick, dark bush, into its tight, slippery channel, all the way until the head of his giant organ hit bottom and she squealed with the exquisite joy of new, fresh discovery.

Neither was in any hurry, though their eagerness was tearing at them. He began to move slowly inside her as she met his rhythm, following his dance, a perfect partner.

She drew her knees up, arching her back and wiggling her hips so that he reached her even more deeply; then she moved more quickly, but always allowing him to lead, following his indications for the particular rhythm.

Then the moment came when neither could any longer have a say in the matter; the lovemaking itself took over as they succumbed to its dictates, moving in perfect harmony with each other, and, when changing position, it was the lovemaking that decided it. The happy lovers simply obeyed their tremendous, stroking passion.

"God, God—" Her murmurs were almost inaudible against his ear, her tongue darting out like a butterfly to drive him to even further ecstasy. Finally, neither could contain it, and indeed, they had long since given up even trying to. They were completely immersed in the great joy of their bodies flailing into each other as their rhythm increased and became faster, and faster and faster and faster—then exploded into absolutely nowhere, unless—it flashed through Slocum's mind— you could call it heaven.

They lay on their backs looking up at the sun, the come drying on their bodies, their hands clasped together, his left and her right.

"My God, my God—" she murmured.

"I love your picnic, young lady," he said.

She turned to him and gently bit his ear. "I love your ears."

"I love your—everything," he said, and his hand touched her thigh.

"You set me on fire."

"Me, too," Slocum said. "But you sure know how to put the fire out."

"I never want it to go out," she said. "Not with you." And then, "I didn't mean that. I'm sorry."

"Why are you sorry?"

"I didn't mean to get heavy on you. I don't really feel that; it just popped out."

"Don't be sorry. It's nice."

"You're not the type to settle down. I can tell. So we'll say no more about it."

She sat up suddenly and then swung over on top of him, straddling his body as her firm, upturned breasts brushed his face. And his organ sprang to total rigidity.

She stayed arched above him, teasing his mouth with her nipples, dancing them away as he tried to suck, and finally, when he caught, she squealed with joy.

But now she did the same dance with her hips, brushing her magnificent bush back and forth on the head of his cock, wiggling it and pumping it, while he tried to get it in. Neither yet used their hands, until Slocum could stand it no longer and put his palms up on her pumping buttocks while she, sensing his purpose, circled his erection with her fist and guided it toward her soaking cunt.

Here she teased him, rubbing its head in her moist lips, but not yet allowing full entry. But she gave way to his hands pressing her undulating buttocks and now allowed the head of his cock to come farther in.

Teasing, he drove it in and then pulled almost all the way out, while she gasped in total joy. Now she reached down and held his thrusting buttocks, drawing him in as he sucked her right breast, then her left; then found her mouth, sinking his tongue deep into it, while she played her own tongue with his.

In this way they rode each other until, in perfect unison, they came, and came—and came—

In the big front room at the Elk Saloon, the game was jackpot poker. This required a pair of jacks or better to open. The dealer was an olive-skinned man with a thin mustache and a habit of sucking his teeth loudly between each draw.

It was clear to Slocum that the dealer was no professional in the more honorable sense of the word, but fit more under the description of tinhorn. His name was Joe Tony, and Slocum had a thin, nagging sense of something familiar about the man. Yet, for the moment, he couldn't place him. The West, after all, was full of such tinhorns, not very good gamblers whose habits gave the gaming tables a bad name. Of course, Slocum fully realized, it was even more so with the so-called "gunslingers"; men who laid claim to skill with the handgun. More often than not, they had gained their reputations through backshooting, ambush, or other trickery. But that was another story, he told himself.

Right now, Slocum realized that the dealer was bent on slickering the young kid sitting across from him, a young cowpoke, with a lot of yellow hair, a big hat with a brim almost wider than his shoulders, and a very earnest expression on his otherwise cheerful face. At the same time, standing directly behind him, Slocum spotted the young boy named Red who had attempted to defend the honor of the skinny girl named Clementine Jones in the Only Time Saloon not very long ago. It appeared that Red, who was drooling a little at a corner of his mouth and now and again rolling his eyes strangely, was trying to befriend the young cowboy, for he kept talking to him, though he received little attention, except once being told to shut up.

But Slocum could see that the play was "in"; the dealer was going to jam the cowboy. It had started early in the game when thin-eyed, thin-lipped Joe Tony began delivering comments on the young man's way of handling the cards. The cowboy, Slocum decided, couldn't have been much more than nineteen, maybe twenty at most, but all the same, he appeared pretty sure of himself. He was a no-nonsense young fellow with wide-set eyes and an open face, broad shoulders, and a square jaw. Slocum took a liking to him, as he had indeed to Red, the boy who wasn't quite all there, though he'd been there enough to stand up for the love of his life, Miss Clementine Jones.

Slocum had no intention of interfering with the unfolding scene. The young fellow had to learn the hard way; it was the very best teacher if you had any wish to survive west of the Mississippi.

"Don't have to stare them spots off of yer cards do ya, sonny?"

Joe Tony's sneer cut across the table like a whip, bringing a flush to the young cowhand's face.

"I reckon I'll take what time I need, mister," the young fellow replied.

Slocum smiled at that point, remembering himself at that age, full of piss and vinegar. But he quickly spotted how the redheaded lad was growing more agitated, as he obviously picked up on Joe Tony's animosity toward his friend, the cowboy.

Slocum stood quietly where he was now, every once in a while letting his eyes go to the big mirror behind the bar in order to see who might have entered the saloon. He was watching the game closely, which meant he was watching the players. He had felt something tight when he'd walked into the Elk, and, in fact, he'd felt it the moment he'd ridden into town, after his short trip out to the site of the stage holdup where the five men had been murdered. But he'd found nothing there that seemed especially helpful, other than verification of the fact that there had indeed been an ambush and six horsemen had attacked the coach.

In the saloon, he had heard guarded conversations with careful references to the troubled times, or the need for the law, but no one was singing any loud song. He had casually asked the thin bartender if anybody had been caught, or if the killers were known, and the man had replied with a laconic negative and moved away. Shortly, Slocum had spotted the bartender looking him over from where he was standing at the far end of the bar. A warning note rang through him, and he decided things were going to get raunchy. It was then he'd decided to watch the poker game, hoping that he might pick up on some news from either the players or the onlookers.

The young cowhand still didn't seem to see that the dealer was rigging the game. Slocum had spotted him right off. He studied the other players, but his interest centered back onto Joe Tony and his victim.

The room was crowded. He overheard some references to the holdup and the killings, but nothing useful to him. The ceiling was low, and the air, as somebody remarked, could have been cut into chewing pieces. The whole room stank of whiskey, tobacco, men, and stale clothing.

It was getting into the afternoon, yet the crowd never seemed to abate. The noise increased: the rattle of the two wheels of fortune on the walls, the voices of the cardplayers as they placed their bets, the voices of the men at the long, wide mahogany bar. And through it all, the feeling of uneasiness grew in him. There was something weird, something off, something—

At a pause in the game while drinks were being addressed, Slocum took another look at the noisy room. Then he snapped his attention back to the poker table, and he realized that Joe Tony's sort of careless ineptitude had a purpose. It was apparent that he was trying to pick a fight with the young man in the huge Stetson hat. At the same time, there was something at the back of Slocum's mind telling him he had to watch it. There was something more going on than the obvious.

Suddenly, the cowboy leaned forward heavily on the table and threw his cards angrily into the discard pile.

"You're dealing seconds!" He glared at the dealer, with both his hands lying on the table in front of him.

"You calling me!" Joe Tony's words fell like a whip onto the cards, the money, the baize top on the round table. The room was suddenly much quieter, and at the card table there was total silence.

"I am saying you dealt that queen from the bottom." The cowboy's words were just as hard as those of the older man.

One of the players said, "Why not just play the hand over." He was instantly glared down by the dealer, but then suddenly Joe Tony nodded his small head. "All right then. We'll deal 'em over. But sonny there better watch his big mouth." He looked around at the other players and at the crowd that had gathered. "I want you all to hear this, see what happened. This man, this green kid, he has insulted my good name."

Nobody said anything to that, and the silence grew. But now somebody said they should make it a new deck, and the dealer reached for a new, unopened pack of cards.

The cowboy nodded, while behind him Red Langley shook his head in agreement—at least that was how Slocum saw it—and mumbled some words that were slurred, wet, and incomprehensible.

"Deal 'em then," the cowboy said.

There was a heavy sneer on Joe Tony's face as his eyes roved over the crowd, looking for affirmation. But the faces were impassive. Only Slocum knew that the man had made his point. He had been unjustly accused, as indeed he had planned, and on the next move he'd go all the way.

Joe Tony shuffled, cut, and dealt. The game resumed; the other players remained silent, intent on their own cards, expectant and careful.

On the next hand, the cowboy raked in a modest pot, laying down a straight. At just that moment, Slocum caught something that he had noticed when the little dealer was looking at the crowd. It had happened twice. For just a split second, the little man's eyes had flickered when he looked at Slocum. It had been so quick that it would normally have gone unnoticed. But right now, Slocum remembered it. At the same moment, the dealer suddenly pushed his chair back, his hands dropping below the table.

"Sonny, you didn't have two jacks there before the bets started."

"I sure did."

"You know you got to have jacks or better to play this game."

"I said I did!" The cowboy's voice rose and the room suddenly stopped.

Slocum saw Joe Tony's eyes flicker as his right arm tightened and he leaned forward with his hands beneath the table.

"You're a lying sonofabitch, a goddam cheat!" His words landed like bullets in the waiting room.

And then Slocum saw it. It was quicker than thought, quicker than a flash of light. They must have forgotten the mirror, the fools, for it was there he saw the man in the black shirt come in with his two partners. It was at the moment that the music swelled through the suddenly opened door to the dancing room that the three entered. The same three he'd braced at the Trail Inn. Some sixth sense had ignited the entire saloon, for men had hit the floor; others had thrown themselves out of the range of fire. Even so, there were still others who stayed frozen in their seats or on their feet, with a drink in their hand. The three visitors drew.

But Slocum was ahead. He had hit the floor, drawing as he went down; drawing against the center figure in the mirror, and spinning and firing his big Navy Colt even before he hit the floor. He drilled his man right in the chest. His next shot caught the man on the left in the neck, while he felt the singing cut of a bullet that grazed his left arm.

But now the third man had thrown down his gun and raised his arms high. Real high. Slocum was up. He realized he'd also been nicked along his left leg and his boot heel had been cut. Close enough. But the middle gunman was dead, and the companion on his right was severely wounded, while the third of the trio stood visibly shaking, with his hands as high as he could get them.

"Somebody get the sheriff," Slocum said, as he took in the startled face of the young cowboy, the bugging eyes and dropped jaw of Red, and the pewter-colored face of Joe Tony, the dealer of all that mischief.

Or was he? Slocum had other thoughts on it. But just then a voice cut into that desperate tableau.

"The sheriff is right here, mister. Slocum, you are under arrest."

John Slocum knew that what he said next went nowhere, yet it had to be said. "Sheriff, I shot in self-defense. Those three men tried to bushwhack me. There are witnesses—"

"Any witness who wants to speak up, step forward." Sheriff Miles Hammer stood hard in the space that had cleared around the scene. He was holding a cut-down double-barreled shotgun. A few voices started up, including the cowboy who Joe Tony had tried to slicker, and Red, the boy with the shock of flaming red hair.

"You'll get your day before the judge," the sheriff snapped, cutting them off. "And there ain't that many of you. Two, three. Huh!" His eyes swept the frozen room, then returned to his prisoner. "But I'm not arresting you for just this, Slocum. I'm also arresting you for the holdup of the Five Butte stage and the murder of its passengers."

Slocum felt it then like a punch in his guts. A kind of accelerated sigh went through the room. Of course. But of course. The whole thing had been to set him up, not the cowpoke. And the words that the sheriff of Bounty now added did nothing to mitigate the tight spot he was in.

"And we know that the stage was held up by John Slocum."

"Mind if I ask how you come to know that, Sheriff?" Slocum asked as he laid his gun on the nearest tabletop; the sheriff having signaled with his double-barreled shotgun that he do so.

"How I know that. Why, I've got a letter here from John Slocum saying that's just what he was planning on doing."

"I want to see that!"

"That is court evidence. You'll get a look at it later, when the judge says so."

"Do you know there are two John Slocums in this town, Sheriff?"

"I know. But there is only one now. You just killed the other one. That leaves you, Slocum. And this!" He tapped his shirt pocket.

"But that isn't my handwriting."

"You'll get a chance to prove that. And besides, you could easy as not got somebody to write it so's to hide your writing. Now let's get on down to my jail."

Slocum looked around the room. There were mostly men and they did not look friendly.

"I might be saving you from a rope necktie, Slocum. So get moving." And the sheriff of Bountyville waved his double-barreled .12 gauge. "You men stand back. This here prisoner is going to by God get a fair trial, even if he did by God murder those innocent men and commit more than a few other killings and crimes around the country here." He motioned the barrels of the shotgun toward Slocum. "Get moving now. Out the door and head to the right. And you men—" Raising his voice. "You behave yourselves. This prisoner here; he is innocent till he is proved guilty."

"Which won't take more time than it takes a prairie dog to lick his left ball, by God!" someone intoned, and this was followed by a round of appreciative laughter.

Suddenly Red Langley was standing next to Slocum. "He—he—helped th-th-this—f-f-friend—mine f-f-f-frenn—" And he reached out and grabbed Slocum by the arm.

"Better let me go, son. But thanks." Slocum nodded, smiled, and started out of the room.

Miles Hammer followed, the shotgun ready for any sudden move. Red half ran, stumbling after the small party as the crowd opened to give them passage.

"Somebody clean up this mess here," shouted the bartender as the group went through the swinging doors. "Somebody get Henry, and somebody get a doctor."

"Too late for a doctor, except for him," said someone, pointing at the gunman whom Slocum had shot in the neck. "He needs Doc. Him there—" He nodded at the corpse, at the man whose real name was Easton, but who had called himself John Slocum. "He don't."

"Hell, what we need is a priest," the young cowboy said, looking with disgust at Joe Tony and his grisly part in the setup. For the fact that it had been a setup was now clear to everyone in the room. But it was also clear as daylight that no one was going to say so.

6

The difference between Noah Borrocks and his men was simply that Borrocks had infinitely more cunning. And he made good use of this advantage. At the same time, he was physically superior to any of his band. This was certainly a help when one had to deal with the rougher types who seemed to come from so many of the out-of-the-way communities of that time and place. Faraway areas where the law had not yet dug itself in, and where now the gullible immigrants, collected by the agents sent to Europe by the railroads with promises of the good life, and free land in the West, had brought a swiftly increasing population. Upon this honest and frequently credulous group of hardworking men and women seeking a new life, the road agents, bandits, petty thieves, murderers, and dishonest promoters, con men and medicine hawkers thrived, like the Rocky Mountain ticks that filled themselves with the blood they sucked from the horses, cattle, and other animals.

Certain persons, however, did not allow this flourishing sport to thrive beyond a certain point. In Montana, up around Bannack and Virginia City, "Granny" Stuart had organized the vigilantes, and Cap Williams and X. Biledler had led the men who had wiped out the Plummer gang.

But the road agents were resilient; those who hadn't attended their own necktie party in turn became "vigilantes," though of a different color. These protectors of the cattlemen, the farmers, and the townspeople found a new bonanza in selling "protection" to the more honest, and therefore, in their view, weaker citizens. Men such as Hank Plummer in Virginia City and Hendry Brown in Kansas, posing as sheriffs—and indeed, duly elected and popular—had run the renegades with one hand and the law with the other.

Noah Borrocks, a former member of Plummer's Innocents, as rumor had it, had learned his calling under a master. And now he even polished himself with the notion that he had improved on his teacher. At any rate, he was still alive and free, and he fully intended to remain so.

Borrocks—and he had spread the rumor himself— was said to have ridden with Bloody Bill Anderson. This was true insofar as he had actually ridden with Bloody Bill, though not on any of his more notable escapades. All the same, the Bloody Bill aura had been stamped on him. And he did his best to live up to it. Someone—long forgotten or likely dead—had once remarked that Noah Borrocks surely had no trouble in doing so. He delighted in his image, and was always working at polishing it. In his line of work, it paid off. Indeed, one of his most noted actions was blowing the head off a retired Union colonel who, during the war, had opposed him in a military encounter; the revenge being exacted with a cut down .12 gauge shotgun at extremely close range, a witness stating that the two men had been close enough to shake hands, though they actually hadn't, for the load of buckshot hit the colonel from the rear.

Noah Borrocks delighted in such stories. And to be sure, these followed him wherever he went. The stories had attracted the attention of Mr. Hoving Clime, who had been deeply shocked to discover that the perpetrator of these infamous deeds was presently residing not far from Bountyville, at a hidden retreat in the high mountains to the north, not far from the Canadian border.

Clime was shocked, but Clime was also a realist. And while perhaps reacting verbally to certain situations he from time to time ran into in his life, such as the proximity of a dangerous and low type of person such as Noah Borrocks, he at the same time realized that there was little that could be done about such a circumstance. The man would assuredly prey on his gathering flock. Clime decided that the best approach to the problem was to make good use of the situation. Thus, he had invited Mr. Borrocks to a luncheon at his recently rebuilt stone house.

Hoving Clime, however, understood that he had one tremendous advantage over the man he planned to meet: While Borrocks was a strong man with a strong group of men around him at his every command, Clime, on the other hand, had on his side the Lord. He remembered the last time he had a similar encounter. In that instance, dealing with the fabled road agent Morley Stokes, he had also relied on the Lord and so had been confident, unafraid, and had come through an otherwise desperate situation with flags flying. He expected the same with Borrocks. For it was simply out of the question that having come all this way to establish his dream colony, that an upstart road agent would foil him. After all, it was he, Hoving Clime, who had the real, the moral strength on his side. All that was necessary was to convince Mr. Borrocks of this truth.

The luncheon took place in Clime's territory, Bountyville. Clime wore his usual dark clothes for the occasion, but this time he also wore a white clerical collar about his neck. As an additional weapon in his armory he had Callie play the role of hostess. Borrocks arrived with two armed men, but the luncheon took place without them; Caligula Smith—Callie—making that arrangement quite plain to the three gentlemen the moment they arrived.

Borrocks had never met anyone like Callie—in fact, few had, for Hoving Clime had rather made her over, from a dance-hall hostess to a lady of mysterious background. He had, in a word, educated her to be as he wanted her to be. It had been a delightful undertaking for the two of them, juiced by their extraordinary physical attraction to each other. The only other initial detail to be taken care of had been Clime's wife Marlene, who was presently running the kitchen. Marlene, like so many of the men and women around Hoving Clime, simply and more or less honestly believed that the man had "something very special," and that by helping him, they were furthering God's cause; even more important, though never mentioned, they believed they were storing up riches in Heaven for themselves.

The meeting with Borrocks had been a success; each party privately understood that the benefits that could accrue for himself would be great. That was to say, territory and modus operandi had been mapped and agreed upon.

The luncheon had taken place in the early spring. This July morning, with the sunlight washing over the newly risen town of Bountyville—"anointing us each blessed morning!" as Clime intoned to his congregation—the man who had created a new community, who had brought the message of hope and happiness to the heart of each and every parishioner under his hand, sat at his ease reviewing the great work that he had wrought. He sat behind his big desk, facing the great sky and the tops of some buildings, for his stone house was on higher ground than the rest of Bountyville.

Seated nearby was the sheriff of Bountyville and also Lords Town, a new and still small yet growing community on the other side of the creek that ran along the south side of Bountyville. Lords Town had been named by Hoving Clime in memory of the original hamlet on which Bountyville now stood. It had been necessary to give Miles Hammer something more, and so he had given him this addition to his fief.

Yet, Miles Hammer was not happy with the new arrangement that Clime had made, bringing Borrocks into the picture. In short, deputizing the whole of the Borrocks's gang along with its leader irked him, for he felt it as a threat. He had much preferred Clime's earlier strategy of arresting certain malefactors and, as part of their payment toward the society they had wronged, requiring them to work off their punishment through community service and, of course, contributions of legal expense money to the sheriff's office as well.

Depending on their abilities, they could serve as deputy lawmen or work at carpentry, horse shoeing, and other jobs, as long as they did not upset the economic balance of law abiding individuals or the comminity as a whole. It had gone without saying that the Clime house and its private stable, newly constructed from scratch, had been a result of this form of indentured labor. At the same time, it was a good score toward Hoving Clime's reputation as a noted and devoted builder of the West.

The sheriff of Bountyville and Lords Town was not at all displeased with the arrangement at the start, but with the influx of gunslingers into the town in such generous numbers, it had become a burden which he was finding more and more difficult to carry. He had wanted three or four, maybe a half dozen men, but not more. Decidedly, the most difficult aspect had been the person of Noah Burrocks.

Miles was saying so right now, as he sat stiffly in the deep chair that faced Hoving Clime's big desk.

"But you miss the point, Hammer. You have totally missed the point. Now that you have arrested Slocum, you will very much need Borrocks."

Miles Hammer stared at Clime open-mouthed. "Huh?" At the same time, the sheriff was aware of the fact that Clime had called him Hammer and not Miles.

"You will have Slocum on your hands," Clime went on to explain. "That can be an asset, or it can be an enormous pain in the neck."

"It is a fuckin' pain in the ass!" grumbled the sheriff.

"Whatever part of the anatomy it antagonizes, it is nonetheless a matter that must be dealt with adroitly and immediately. The prisoner Slocum is a fact of life. May I say that all of you followed our most recent plan with unbelievable stupidity. However, we will discuss that presently; that is, later." And his face darkened. "In any case, that crazy boy almost wrecked everything on his own without your help."

"Slocum came close to wrecking everything," said the sheriff. "If I hadn't been right there to arrest him just when I did, he'd have gotten away slick as a whistle."

"Possibly. Possibly." Clime's voice was tight with patience that he did not feel. He was obviously forcing himself to endure the pedestrian understanding of Miles Hammer. Why was the man so slow to follow? Always!

"You see, sir," Clime went on, his words just beginning to congeal, "you realize that everything was playing into our—my—hands. As I planned it. All you had to do was follow the instructions I laid out for you." Clime's large eyes bore—like nails—into Miles Hammer's face. "The point is, I must be certain—you understand me!— absolutely certain that Slocum is not working with the law; that he has *nothing* at all to do with the law!"

"That's what I bin doin'," Hammer insisted bullishly. "Following your instructions. He's in my jail. He can't escape, leastways not without a helluva lot of help. And I laid it out to him. He is caught cold and he's gonna have to deal. He understands that. He ain't dumb."

"You have men guarding him, I trust," Clime said coolly.

"I got two good men with orders to shoot to kill if he tries making a break for it. The two of them would personally like to kill the sonofabitch. They were with Easton when Slocum backwatered 'em at the Trail Inn."

"Good then. So what is the difficulty?" Clime had begun looking at some papers on his desk, making it clear to Hammer that he was busy, and the conversation had gone on long enough.

"So what do you want done now?" the sheriff of Bountyville and Lords Town asked.

"I want him to cool his time there tonight. Maybe another day, or even two. Though we don't have all that much time available."

"What's the hurry?" Hammer asked. "None of us is going anywheres, far as I can see. 'Ceptin' maybe yerself." And then he added, feeling somehow unsure, "But 'course I dunno about that."

"We have a certain amount of time to get something done," Clime explained. "But we needn't go into it, now. And anyway, all you have to do, Miles, is follow instructions. Yes? Keep a tight watch on Slocum. Report to me on anything you or your guards notice as strange. And be sure he doesn't have any contact with anyone outside. You understand, I want him to be absolutely alone! How strong is your jail?"

"It's a log cabin out back of the office. But it's impossible to break out of it, and anyways, we can easy enough chain him to a big log in the middle of the cabin if we got to. He ain't going anywheres."

Suddenly, Clime leaned forward. "I expect to be giving my first sermon in my new church within a month." And he was smiling.

"That'll be something!" And Miles Hammer tried to look happy.

"But this town has to be tamed. And the country about, too," Clime went on. "By jingo, we pacified the damn redskins, now we find we have to pacify our own Americans. It's weird. It is weird, Miles."

"What do you mean?" Hammer asked, his expression emphasizing the fact that he was clearly puzzled.

"I mean, we Americans pioneered this land. We established ourselves here under tremendous difficulties. Unimaginable dangers!" He held high his forefinger to emphasize his point. "And the noble, brave men and women fought the natives, subdued them; subdued the wilderness, harnessed nature for man's benefit, no less! Defeated the enemy—the British, the French, the Spanish, and the Dutch, and as already stated, the redskins. Why—hah! You know it makes me laugh, Hammer. Miles!"

"What makes you laugh?" And Miles Hammer suddenly wondered if Clime might have been drinking. "I don't see anything to laugh about. I think we've got our hands too damn full! But I'm not complaining. I'm not at all complaining! I'm only wondering what you find to laugh about."

"I'm talking about Borrocks, of course. He is always talking about how he rode with Wild Bill Sanderson."

"Well, that's not nothing, I'd allow," said Hammer, swiftly getting a few words into the conversation that was mostly rolling off Climes's smooth and ready tongue. "And it's Bloody Bill, not Wild!"

"But, by God man. Who the devil was this Wild Bill or Bloody Bill Sanderson! Why I—"

"Anderson!" Hammer cut in. "Not Sanderson. Bloody Bill Anderson!"

"Hell's bells, Man! Why yours truly rode with Chivington! Colonel John M. Chivington, Sir! Put that in your pipe and smoke it!"

"You mean you were in on that massacre at Sand Creek?"

"It was not a massacre, sir. But we wiped out the heathen savages, thus making the country safe for the settlers, the women and children who wanted to till the land and raise their crops and their children in the light of the Lord!"

"I heerd Chivington and his men massacreed the old men, all of who wuz unarmed, plus the women and children. And the Injuns was peaceful flying a American flag over the chief's tepee, and all!"

Too late, Miles Hammer realized he had forgotten himself, and he stopped cold, his face flushed with argument; not that he cared all that much about the natives, but he was tired of listening to the other man's bragging.

But Clime was as cool as a morning leaf before the sun hit it. "I see. You lose yourself so easily, Hammer. You fool, falling for my little trap. And you think you can handle a man like Slocum! My God, man. He'd make mincemeat out of you! Now, by damn, you might at last see why I have brought Borrocks and his men, and I hope shortly Slocum, into my operation. I need men who can control themselves and can think ahead, Hammer. And you, you don't know how to control yourself."

But Miles Hammer had learned something. He had lost considerable ground; he knew that. But he wasn't going to lose any more. So he stuck to his ground; held his tongue, listened to the lashing, arrogant, domineering, all-knowing tongue of the man he knew he hated more than any other: Hoving Clime.

At the same time, he knew fear as he left the stone house. He had worked hard for his job. He had always wanted to be a lawman, and he had finally succeeded. By God, he sure didn't go for that holy sonofabitch with his big-belly-know-it-all ways and fast talk. But he was in a fix. And how the hell he was going to get out was something else. But first things first. He was in the middle. And the best thing to do was to get the hell out of the middle fast.

Slocum lay on the foul bedding on the floor of the cabin located behind the sheriff's office at one end of town, a good distance from the residents, but near two saloons, and he could hear occasional sounds of the high living going on.

It was a one-room log cabin that served as the jail, a low structure, and one had to step down about two feet upon entering. The inside smelled rancid with the stink of old skillet grease thrown on the dirt floor to settle the dust. The furniture consisted of the potbellied stove, which had evidently been used in the past as a kitchen range, hence the grease; a wooden chair with no back; and a heavy table, on which two tallow candles sat in their own wax amid myriad scars as though the table had been used for carving meat, cutting wood, or simply for wanton cutting and stabbing with a knife.

The walls were unpeeled cedar logs with mud and manure chinking, the roof was simply a solidly thick, flat layer of boughs, sod, and manure; the floor was hardpan. The door was of new, heavy lumber, pad-locked on the outside. There was no window and very little light, unless he used the candles. A minimum of daylight did filter in through some of the many chinks. As far as Slocum was concerned, it was no place to spend any length of time. Clearly, the only way to escape would be to overpower his two large and heavily armed guards, one of whom always waited outside while his companion came in with food or water.

He wondered if they wanted him to escape so that they would have an excuse to cut him down. But that thought went nowhere. No, he was sure they wanted him alive. They had taken his six-gun and Bowie knife, which had been strapped to his leg. There was an outhouse behind the cabin, to which they escorted him when he called. The only way he could make a run for it would be during that time. But his guards were not dreamy. And so it would simply be a question of waiting; the next move would be up to whoever had planned the situation.

Lying on his bedding, he found himself thinking of Annie Gilchrist and hoping that nobody had been bothering her because of him, although they had been careful about being seen together. He wondered, too, about Terence at the Trail Inn, who would see that he wasn't there, and would hear of the fracas in the Elk Saloon. He even found himself thinking about Red, the nervous young man with the flaming red hair, and his skinny girlfriend. He wondered, too, if whoever had worked him into this jam was also looking to squeeze anyone he'd been seen with. It depended, of course, on just what they wanted from him.

Slocum had heard more details on the vigilante angle from Gulley: that Sheriff Hammer was keeping the men he arrested in jail until they agreed to become deputies. Were they pushing him toward that? Maybe in part it was that. But he felt that there was more to it. Why had there been the man Easton, claiming he was John Slocum?

And why did anyone want him in the first place?

And the man Borrocks, the chief of the Regulators. He had heard of Borrocks—

And who the hell was Clime?

It had been a big question with Slocum why the men who had shot and all but lynched Gulley had not made another attempt. He had argued with the old boy that he accompany him to see Sheriff Miles Hammer, but Gulley had insisted that Hammer was part of the gang that had tried to kill him, and that it would just be walking into the bear's open jaws.

"They'll wait," Gulley had predicted. "See, they just actually, really wanted to scare me. Make sure I didn't talk. I could tell that."

"What do you mean?" Slocum had persisted. "They sure as hell went to some fancy lengths for a threat."

"A threat, like I said," Gulley insisted.

"Some threat, if I hadn't come along."

Gulley had shrugged. "In the old days, they wouldn't a one of them or even a dozen have dared mess with a Tyrone."

"What old days?"

"When I was a strapping lad. One tough, mean sonofabitch, by God!"

"Huh," Slocum said.

"Lemme tell ya, I was a tough boy. Challenged Yankee Sullivan for the champeenship. Bugger was afraid of me, he was. I knocked out two men what beat him. Ya know that!" He almost started up from his chair, but sat back, as though remembering something. "Have ya heard of this young new feller now, also named Sullivan?"

"The Boston fighter?"

"That's him. John L. He just whipped Paddy Ryan. I tell you, if I was ten years younger, I'd challenge him. Thinks he's hot shit, he does. Let me tell you, they don't make the fighters like they used to."

"How's that?" Slocum asked, hoping to get the old boy to open up, which in fact was the purpose of his visit.

"Too soft. They're all of 'em soft." He cleared his throat, but before he could spit, he was overcome by a gigantic sneeze. With a growl of displeasure, Theodore, lying close by, shifted his position, the end of his orange tail curling in retaliation for the rude disturbance to his nap.

"So, what you getting hot under the collar for? Nobody's allowed to sneeze in his own house, that it?"

The man and the cat glared at each other, but Theodore had the last—even though silent—word, as he arched his back, then stretched and strode magnificently across the room and lay down in a second spot of sunlight, which now mantled him as his eyes closed in total self-satisfaction.

"You should move out of here," Slocum said. But the old man sniffed, shook his head, and said nothing.

"Give me one good reason for not leaving." Slocum insisted. Though he knew the answer, he wanted to hear the old man say it.

"On account of my daughter. On account of I ain't the runaway type, goddamn it. And on account of, if they was gonna kill me this time, they'd've done so already."

Slocum nodded. "All right. I agree with you. I agree they would have hit you again, except I've been staying pretty close, just in case you hadn't noticed."

Gulley mumbled something inarticulate, and the matter had been dropped.

Sitting cross-legged on his bedding in the town jail, Slocum reviewed the scene, realizing there was something irresistible about old Gulley. Gulley had told him that he could—when he was younger, and by God maybe even now—whip any man in the house. "Gulley Tyrone can lick anything walking on two legs. 'Specially when he's had himself his ration of whiskey!"

Slocum had come pretty close to believing him. Nevertheless, he knew the old boy wasn't all that good.

And if the men who had shot him off the stage came after him again, they wouldn't make another mistake like the last one—if it had indeed been a mistake. No matter. Next time they'd make sure he was dead before they left him; it wouldn't be just another threat.

Which made him lean closer to the notion that they were indeed actually aiming to frighten Gulley. After all, it seemed sure it had been information they sought. They had put it in the way that had suggested they were afraid of his talking to someone else about something he knew about the gang. But in reality, it could have been that they were really interested in getting information about something else out of him. But what? Had they been planning to come back to the scene of the "lynching" to see if by then he would tell them what they wanted to know?

It simply didn't make sense. No, they had wanted to kill him right then and there, and they had wanted him to suffer for it. They had not urged him to tell them anything.

Or had they? The argument kept changing sides. Gulley had said they hadn't asked him any questions; and even though Slocum had pressed him on it, he'd stuck to his story. They hadn't asked him anything. They had just said he wouldn't be talking to anyone. About what?

Gulley had insisted to Slocum that he didn't know. And so for the present, Slocum had taken him at his word. He saw no reason why the old man would lie to him. And, too, it could be that the lynching party had even changed its mind. Anyway, they knew now, of course, that he had escaped the noose they'd so carefully prepared for him, and they could have easily killed him at any moment; but maybe—maybe they had simply botched the whole thing; it could be as simple as that.

He let it go. Too much woolgathering wasn't good for you. And he had to put all his attention on his own situation. He was not in the happiest place he'd ever been in. And he had no promise or anticipation that it was going to get any better.

The thing to do now was to figure a way of escape. He had been here a day and a night now, and as near as he could figure by his inner timepiece, it had to be early morning. He had just pulled his boots on and was standing, stretching his body a little, for he'd been lying on hardpan, when he heard the key in the padlock.

When the door was pushed open one of his two jailers walked in. It was Bruce, and Slocum heard the other guard, Ketchum, talking to somebody outside.

The next thing Slocum knew, Gulley Tyrone had been pushed into the cabin. His hands were tied behind his back, and Slocum immediately saw the glint of fresh blood on his forehead.

"It was that fool Easton bungled it," Miles Hammer insisted as he stood, bareheaded and tense, in front of Hoving Clime. "Figured to build hisself a reputation."

It was morning, and the sun breaking through the window of Clime's office did little to relieve the atmosphere of tension, anger, and fear that inhabited that tight room.

Clime was standing behind his desk, leaning forward a little, the pads on the ends of his thick, stubby fingers pressing into his scattered papers. He was looking down, his eyes on the Bible which was always at hand. But he didn't see it.

"You Goddamned fools!" The voice, soft as the whisper of silk, cut into the man standing in front of him. "You idiots! Do you realize what you've done?"

"Like I told you, it was Easton." The sheriff of Bountyville and Lords Town was dangling. He was thanking God Easton was dead. Slocum had done a good turn.

"You mean, Easton is the scapegoat for your blundering! And Borrocks!" The voice was no longer soft. It had risen swiftly during those two statements and now ended in a roar. "You stupid sonsofbitches! Goddamn you! Goddamn you! God double damn you to hellfire!"

"Hoving—"

"Do *not* speak to me with your filthy familiarity, Sheriff! You will address me in the proper way, either as Mr. Clime, or possibly, as a hint toward a better path, as Reverend Clime. You stupid sonofabitch!"

Miles Hammer's face had definitely darkened, but he held his tongue. Clime took note. He had pushed it as far as he could for the moment. Well and good.

"Sit."

Hammer was a brave man, but he was mightily relieved to find a chair beneath him. He looked carefully at the man seated behind the big desk. To his amazement, he saw a quite different Hoving Clime. The man was no longer in a raging fury, almost spitting his words, looking as though he was ready to kill. Now he was a calm, cool, collected gent— the reverend, for Christ's sake!—with that shit-eating smile on his goddamn face. These were the thoughts slipping into the sheriff's bitter mind. Well, maybe the bad moment was passing.

Now the voice was calm, reasonable. "Look, I explained it to you, to Borrocks, and also to Easton.

It was very simple. Don't you remember it?" He didn't
wait for an answer, but went on. "Let's take it from
the beginning. I *wanted* you to frighten Tyrone, not
kill him. He could easy as not have been killed when
you shot him off the stage. Do you realize how close
you three came to wrecking my entire plan? No. And
do you know why you don't realize this?" The voice
was now as calm as a plate of water. Reverend Clime,
as he now more frequently chose to be called, might
as easily have been discussing the beatitudes. "Yes,
Hammer; Sheriff Hammer, I should say—yes, indeed.
You do not understand why you did not realize this
simple fact; that it was necessary—nay, essential—not
to do anything more than frighten the old man. But you
goddamn fools came within an ace of killing him!" The
voice had suddenly charged out of the man behind the
desk, like a train roaring out of a tunnel with its whistle
screaming and its headlight glaring.

Clime was suddenly purple, gasping for air. Reaching
up, he loosened his collar. "Very well. So all right, calm!
Let us be calm!" He stopped, his stertorous breathing
the only sound in the room. Clime's eyes, appearing
to Miles Hammer like two large eggs, regarded him
solemnly. "Calm," Clime repeated; though there was
no way of knowing whether he was saying this to
himself or to the sheriff.

"We will start over once more from the beginning,
Miles. Now listen carefully." He leaned back, drumming
his fingers on the desktop. "To begin with, you have
arrested both Slocum as well as the old boy—" He
looked down, suddenly searching his memory and
drumming his fingers on the desk. "Gulley. Yes,
Tyrone. You have them both in your little hotel behind
your office."

"That's about the size of it."

"Release them."

The sheriff's forehead broke into a series of deep wrinkles. "Release 'em?"

"That is correct." The voice was menacingly patient. "Listen carefully, Miles. Release them, saying that a certain person had heard of their predicament and had come to see you asking for their release. You got that?"

The sheriff's mouth dropped open. He nodded, obviously not understanding the nuances that were inside Clime's words.

"You will not tell them right away who it was who cobbled together this kind deed, but they may question you, and if so, then you will let them find out. But do not go out of your way to tell them. You understand?"

"I do."

"You sure?"

"I am."

"Be very sure, Miles."

"I am very sure."

A silence entered the room for a moment, and then Hammer said, "Just let 'em go then. No other answers to anything, except who got them out, only if they ask."

"That is correct. I—or one of my men—will take up from that point on." Clime leaned forward now, his elbows on the desk, his hands open. "Miles, you're not asking me why."

"I figgered you'd let me know if and when you wanted," the sheriff said cleverly, though in a sober tone of voice.

"Good then, Miles. You are learning. You see, not only are the ways of the Lord a wonder and mystery to behold; but so, too, is the way of higher intelligence, which, as a matter of obvious fact, is the servant, or perhaps it would be better to say, the messenger of the Eternal Source."

"Jesus!" murmured Hammer, the word barely more than his breath.

But Clime had sharp ears. "No, Miles. Not Jesus. Higher."

Miles Hammer's jaw dropped. He had been about to add "Christ," but just in time, thought better of it.

"The Lord's name must not be taken in vain, Miles. I want you to come to service this Sunday. There is much for you to learn, my man. Much. A very great deal." His eyes lifted, sweeping the ceiling, and for all the sheriff, who was watching him closely, knew, beyond.

"Now then. Back to business." He had changed in a flash, leaving the moment of contact with whatever it was he saw and returning to the secular.

"Then you will have the two of them watched. You see, and let me explain this, Tyrone knows something and I am not sure that he knows he knows it." Seeing the sudden consternation in the other man's face, he said, "Do not utter blasphemy, Miles, but listen. I wouldn't be surprised if Slocum knew this—I mean that he is aware of Gulley Tyrone knowing something but not knowing he knows it."

Suddenly, Hammer's rigid face relaxed. "Got'cha!" He grinned. "You mean like where maybe something is cached! Huh?"

Hoving Clime regarded the man on the other side of his desk with his lids half lowered, the corners of his mouth soft as a small child's, while he opened his hands as though making an offering to the Great Mystery. "We are but the humble servants of a higher will," he said, his tone almost sepulchral. "But if there is any gain awaiting us, then we can be sure that such emolument would go toward our great works here in Bountyville."

The sheriff belched softly, trying to handle his ignorance of some of the other man's vocabulary. Whatever it was, it sounded good, and he had confidence that Clime would carry it off.

Once again, as he left Hoving Clime's presence, he wondered at how he'd gotten involved in whatever it was he was involved in. But he kept in mind that, no matter what it was he was headed for, it was a whole lot better than Laramie or Folsom or any of those other places where you ended up if you didn't keep your nose clean.

The release from the Bountyville jail was conducted with simplicity, secrecy, and almost total silence. The two prisoners had been sitting quietly in the near-dark as evening approached, for there didn't seem to either of them any particular reason to light one of the candle stubs. Besides, there was no way of knowing when they might get another when they ran out.

Gulley had related to Slocum the details of his arrest, and how the two deputies had manhandled him, cutting him over the head with a pistol barrel, and also pistol-whipping his arms for good measure.

Suddenly, the guards were there at the padlock, which was ancient, rusted, and often defied attempts to open it. Finally, after much hitting, cursing, and heavy breathing, someone managed to find the right touch and the padlock opened. Five minutes later, the pair of prisoners were free men.

They stood in Miles Hammer's office, facing the sheriff; the two deputies had departed.

"You're free," Hammer said, his tone laced with disapproval, "but I don't want any more trouble from either one of yez. You got that?"

"No," Slocum said, feeling his gorge rise at the sheriff's insolent attitude. "If there is trouble, it will be—as it was before—on your account, not ours."

Hammer scowled, but remembered he was under orders, so he said nothing. Within minutes, Slocum and his companion were at the bar in the Only Time. Heads had turned as they entered and traversed the room. Cecil, the big bartender, had regarded them as only a bartender serene in the authority of his position was able. He gave no sign of recognition, yet every fiber of his large figure was alert to the slightest nuance of barroom disturbance.

They took their drinks to a table at the far end of the room and sat, Gulley having the presence of mind to include the bottle.

"Looks like word got out already," Slocum said as he downed a good slug. "Aah, that's just what the doc ordered!"

"I ain't arguin' it," his companion said, his sudden sneeze blistering the atmosphere at their table. "How you figger this now, Slocum? I smell a rat, or maybe a skunk."

"Well, the whole setup was in order to put us right here, wouldn't you say?"

"Here? You mean, where we be right now?"

"Right now at this moment."

They paused for another round, Gulley pouring this time. "Lookee there, filled right to the brim without spillin'."

"See if you can drink it without a spill then."

Chuckling, the old boy loosened his shoulders, waggled his elbows, and with a glint in his eye, reached for his whiskey. He held the shot glass for a moment, gazing down at it, and then lifted and downed it. A great gasp blew out of his pursed mouth, his eyes watered, with Slocum receiving the exhaust of his powerful whiskey breath.

"You try it," Gulley said.

The effort was repeated, but now Slocum poured, bringing the brown fluid right to the lip of the shot glass, the same as Gulley had done.

"Now you got to lift her and not lose a whisker," the old man prompted.

"You can say it's as good as done," Slocum replied, as he raised his glass. His hand was still as a stone as he held the whiskey right in front of his eyes.

"Drink 'er then," Gulley said. "What you waitin' fer?"

Slocum had paused, but only for a split second, holding his glass absolutely still, but with his eyes beyond the brown liquid, to the big mirror behind the bar and big Cecil, to the man who had just entered the Only Time.

"Who you see?" Gulley asked, suddenly alert.

"Big fellow," Slocum said, now drinking his whiskey. "And he has seen us. Don't know him, but I'd say ten'll get you twenty it's Borrocks."

"He got one suspender?"

"Yup."

7

The room was thick with cigar smoke, and when Callie walked in, her eyes began to water, and she coughed.

Clime, his back to the door as he bent over the large map that was spread on his desk, straightened and turned.

"My dear, what an exciting moment! I want you to share this with me."

"That man, the one you were talking to, said you wanted to see me." She was looking at him expectantly, her face serene and without expression, except that Clime detected a smile waiting at the corners of her mouth and just behind her eyes. She was wearing her spectacles, which did nothing to detract from her good looks.

"He'll be back in a moment, my dear. I wanted you to see this." His thick middle finger tapped at a place on the map, as he turned his head and, reaching over with his left hand, felt the smooth curve of her buttock.

"Poppy—be careful."

But he caught the delighted intake of her breath as his hand remained.

"Your man will be back."

"Damnit." He dropped his hand and straightened up, but with a look in his eye that made her break into laughter.

"Mister Clime—Reverend, sir, behave yourself. Now what is it you wanted me to see?"

He was on the verge of saying something obscene, but just then Hooligan, the surveyor, came back into the room.

"Aah, Clarence! I'd like to introduce you to Miss Caligula Smith, my—uh—secretary, housekeeper, and also, of course, one of my most trusted."

Clarence Hooligan, a round man with innumerable freckles all over his face, his neck, and the backs of his hands, beamed with pleasure.

"Clarence and I have just been making sure of the boundaries of our—well, let's call it our constituency, my dear. You see—" He pointed on the map. "You see, there will soon be a good bit of circuit riding; for our area has grown." He beamed on the eager Clarence, who nodded vigorously. "Our flock has multiplied beyond all expectations, you see. And of course, you can understand now why it was so necessary to conduct this survey. I am overwhelmed at the work that lies ahead. But—." And he raised his forefinger high. "But the Lord's good work is never done! Ah—" His great head bowed, and both Callie and Clarence Hooligan wondered if he was about to conduct a prayer. Silence filled the room, punctuated by Clarence Hooligan's thin rapid breathing. The man had trouble with the high altitude.

Suddenly, Clime's eye struck at him. "Clarence, you a lunger?" And there was real concern in those words.

"Had trouble all my life with the lungs. 'Specially when I was a boy."

"But this high altitude—?"

"It's s'posed to help it. I dunno." He shrugged his puny, almost invisible shoulders, and Clime suddenly found himself wondering if the surveyor's whole body was as freckled as his face.

And then, with a sudden spasm of jealousy, he looked at Callie and wondered if she was thinking the same thing.

"Well, Clarence, just explain one detail here, will you. Nothing especially to do with the survey of our— uh—diocese; or better, jurisdiction." And leaning over, his thick forefinger pointed at a place on the map.

"There, where your finger's pointing?" Clarence was squinting as he studied the place indicated by Clime.

"Right there."

"There? It looks to be a gulch, and there, a pretty high ledge. That water there, looks like Jackass Creek." Clarence's forefinger traced the line along the paper, looking for a name. "It don't say what it is. Anyway, it is water. That there, where you had your finger, looks like a lot of rock."

"I take it that's within our—uh—boundary. Not that it's important."

"I don't know. I don't think it is, for the matter of that." Clarence's tone was bland, unconcerned.

"I see. Then, what? That's government land then, is it?" he added, when he didn't feel a response coming from Clarence.

"It could be. Or maybe it isn't. It might be your land."

"But the map is the map."

"Yes, but these old maps aren't always the most accurate. You see—"

But Clime stopped him right there. "Clarence, you're not trying to hold me up for an additional fee, are you?"

The Hooligan freckles seemed to run off in all directions as alarm struck, and Clarence's face flushed red, almost scarlet with embarrassment.

"Why no, Mr. Clime. I mean, Reverend. I am only stating that these maps are extremely difficult to draw in the first place, and it's the easiest thing in the world for a mistake to creep in. And not only mistakes, let me add that one of the major difficulties lies in people's inability to read a map."

"I thought I was reading this map fairly intelligently," replied Clime, his tone frosty. "Of course, I am not a surveyor; it's not my profession, but I can read, after all."

" 'Course! Of course!" Clarence's face was almost black with concern at the gaffe he had pulled. But then anger saved the day for him. For, damn it, he was indeed a professional, and he knew his job, and that pompous come-to-Jesus barker couldn't hold a candle to him there, by damn!

But when he looked back at Clime, he couldn't hold it. Clime, he had to admit, well, it was like dealing with a Kansas twister.

"I could check it again," Clarence said, keeping his voice firm, and not giving up much ground. "Though it would probably be easier just to buy the piece."

"But it's not that, my lad! I don't *want* that piece of land. I was just curious, interested; that's all. I have no need for more land. My parish—my constituency—has more than enough land to support its members, and even to add more, let me say!"

"Of course," said Clarence in his most mollifying tone. "Of course. I am sorry. I misunderstood you."

"Though if it isn't any extra trouble, and you've the time, I'd be sincerely interested. You see, there's a creek there."

"You mean water."

"Why, of course."

"I will look into it," Clarence said. "Certainly." And as his embarrassment subsided, and he felt himself growing cooler, he was aware that somehow, in some strange way, he, Clarence Hooligan, a man of no importance whatever, had in spite of himself aced the Reverend Hoving Clime. But with his life on the line he knew he would never, never have even an inkling of how that had happened. Or what it could mean.

The arrival of the man with one suspender had brought the Only Time into a lower key. Silence didn't fall, but voices slowed, as did movements; the atmosphere softened from its brash expression of devil-may-care to an inner, and in a certain way, tighter quality. It would have been no exaggeration to say that caution was the mode. And maybe it was best expressed by the fact that nobody's eyes found anyone else's. At such a time, as Slocum well knew, a man made damn sure he didn't hold anybody's look.

And so, Slocum was thinking, it's Borrocks and his two sidekicks there; and the thought swept through him how certain gunmen favored two companions. Easton, bracing him in the Elk Saloon and in the Trail Inn too, had been sided with heavy artillery, and now Borrocks did the same. But there was a major difference, and there couldn't have been a man in the room who failed to notice it. Borrocks was unarmed.

His companions were not. Each packed a brace of
six-guns, and they were positioned in the customary
place that offered their speediest inclusion into any
passage at arms.

As Borrocks strode to the bar, his two companions
spread out and remained behind him. Slocum took note
of how professionally they had the room covered, with
the unarmed Borrocks as the centerpieces.

Silence. The clink of a glass. Someone sneezed. And
Slocum wondered where Miles Hammer, the sheriff,
might be.

"Whiskey," Borrocks said to the silent figure behind
the bar.

"Just you, Noah?" Cecil placed the glass and bottle
in front of Borrocks, throwing a glance at the two
sidekicks.

Borrocks didn't answer. Plainly, the question required
no answer. But Cecil, an old hand, bore it. Now the room
began to stir. A chair scraped on the floor. There was the
clink of money. And somebody coughed, a long loose
coughing, with much clearing of phlegm and spitting,
followed by a resigned cursing.

Slocum noticed that the two sidekicks didn't move.
Each was close to a wall, opposite each other, but
covering their leader, who relaxed at the bar.

"What the hell's he up to?" Gulley's tone was
low, but not a whisper. Slocum heard him clearly.

"Don't know. You reckon they're looking for somebody?"

A kind of cackle fell from his companion. "Heh!
Could be yerself. What you think?"

"The time has passed. It's something else," Slocum
said. "If it's me, there's no advantage to their waiting.

I'd say the man wasn't here yet; or maybe they're just studying the town."

Meanwhile, Noah Borrocks had turned and was facing the big room, leaning back onto his elbows, which were on the bar.

Just then, the swinging doors opened and Miles Hammer walked into the saloon. Slocum caught the almost imperceptible nod he gave Borrocks who, it was clear now, had been waiting for him.

Then Hammer was standing in front of Slocum and Gulley Tyrone.

"Mister Clime would still like to see you, Slocum." His voice was low, not carrying beyond their table. "I think you ought to go see him."

"So?" Slocum had shifted his position, even before Hammer had come through the swinging doors, so that he would be ready for any action.

"Hell, man, he's the one who saved your ass. Got you out of jail. You wouldn't be settin' here drinking if it warn't fer Mister Clime."

"Tell him I'm obliged," Slocum said.

"You coming along? I'm heading that way."

"Have a nice journey then."

"I could arrest you again."

"What for?"

"You're breaking the law."

"The hell you say!"

"You're packing a gun and that's against the town ordinance."

"When was that put through, about ten minutes ago?"

"Doesn't matter, mister. It's now. It is the law."

"And what about all of them?" Slocum nodded toward the two men who had come in with Borrocks.

"They're deputies. On special duty with him." He

nodded in the direction of Borrocks, who was watching the situation.

"And what about them?" Slocum said, indicating the rest of the saloon. "There's more hardware in this room than you can shake a stick at."

"They're not disturbing the peace."

"That what the law says? You can pack a gun long as you're not disturbing the peace?"

The sheriff nodded. He was standing with his legs slightly apart, his thumbs hooked into his wide belt.

"I'm not breaking any law," Slocum said, though he knew what the answer to that would be.

"You want to come along now to talk with the man who saved you from a necktie party?"

Slocum knew what was coming. If he made any move toward his gun, they'd crossfire him. But why was Borrocks unarmed? He turned his head and looked at the big man, who, still leaning his back against the bar, had his thumb hooked into his single suspender.

"See, he's one of my deputies. Fact, in charge of the Regulators. See, he's settin' a example. This town's got too many guns."

"It has got too damn many bullshit vigilantes," Slocum said. He started to shift in his chair, as though ready to get up, and caught the movement from Borrocks at the bar.

"You comin', Slocum?"

"You can tell Mr. Clime that it'll take just as much time for him to walk here as for me to walk there."

"You're breakin' the law."

"No, I'm not. You and your gang are breaking the law."

"I'm going to have to arrest you 'less you unbuckle that gun."

"You tell him," Slocum said, nodding his head toward Borrocks. "And them." He nodded toward the two men who had entered with Borrocks.

"Borrocks is unarmed," Miles Hammer said. "Hell, you can see that."

"He's got a belly gun under that shirt, and you and I and he know it."

Suddenly, he stood up. "But I see we're getting nowhere with this chin music." He unbuckled his gun, but instead of handing it to the sheriff, he gave it to Gulley. "You want to buy into this hand, Gulley?"

"I bought in the minute I seen them rats crawl in here, friend."

Slocum stood facing the sheriff. "You let them start throwing lead in here, Hammer, you'll have a bloodbath that would stain the Mississippi. Don't be a damn fool, man!"

"Slocum—" But Hammer's voice had no power in it. Slocum had already turned away from him, and in just three or four steps he was standing in front of Noah Borrocks. He had moved so quickly, and with not the least waste of movement, that he was there in front of the head of the Regulators before Borrocks could get set.

"You take that belly gun out of your shirt. I mean right now!"

"Slocum, go fuck yourself!"

But John Slocum had already moved, knowing what Borrocks's answer would be beforehand. And his short driving punch, which he brought all the way from his heel up through his body and into his left fist, landed like a bomb in Borrocks's solar plexus. Borrocks let out a grunt like the sound of a bass drum and bent, his face turning white.

Slocum's next punch was a chopping right brought down on the side of the big man's neck, and Borrocks was flat on his face.

Slocum stood over him. "Get up." He reached down and ripped open Borrocks's shirt and yanked out the hidden gun. Tossing it on top of the bar, he stepped back, letting the big man struggle to his feet.

Borrocks stood there, shaking his head, swaying, hardly able to remain upright it seemed.

"Jeesus, did he clout him!" somebody said with great glee. "That'll show him, by God!"

But Slocum was watching Borrocks closely, and he wasn't fooled. He could tell the man was faking, exaggerating his weakness, and in the next moment, he was proved correct.

But Borrocks didn't attack. Instead, he began retreating across the floor, away from the bar, until he reached a whiskey bottle, which he grabbed and threw at Slocum, who was stalking him. Slocum ducked, and the bottle sailed into the wheel of fortune on the wall behind him.

"Cecil!" The command broke from Borrocks and there was no way the bartender could have denied it.

But Slocum remembered the bung starter from the last fracas he'd attended in the Only Time. Quick as a wink, he charged Borrocks, who now stood his ground and threw a murderous left and right at his opponent. His first blow missed completely, but the second caught Slocum on his temple and nearly turned him around. In the excitement of possibly turning the tables, Borrocks didn't grab the bung starter that Cecil had brought up from behind the bar, but instead, charged Slocum, swinging both hands. His blows were powerful; each fist had the kick of a horse. He landed on Slocum's ear, his neck, and punished him around the kidneys. His attempt at backheeling his opponent failed, and Slocum slammed him in the ribs, kidneys, and in the belly. The big man grunted and gave ground.

He was close to the bar now, and Cecil had the bung starter ready to hand him, when suddenly Borrocks changed his tactics and, grabbing a chair, shoved it at Slocum's feet.

Too late, Slocum tried to avoid it hitting his legs, but he was down, and the big man was on him, with knees, elbows, and thumbs gouging into his eyes. Slocum brought his knee up, slamming Borrocks in the pit of his stomach. The big man grunted, relaxed his grip on Slocum's hair, and Slocum was up on his feet.

Now Slocum had his second wind, and as Borrocks charged, he sidestepped, feinted a left, and brought over a right hook that staggered the vigilante. They faced each other, moving about on their feet, weaving their bodies, looking for an opening. Slocum felt the blood in his nose, and he could see that Borrocks's left eye was swollen almost shut, while his breathing was labored. For half a minute they circled each other, and, as Borrocks passed close to the bar, he grabbed the bung starter that Cecil handed him.

"C'mon, you sonofabitch!" he snarled and swung the deadly weapon like a blade at his opponent.

Slocum ducked, slammed a short right hook into the other man's belly, but received the bung starter between his shoulder blades and was almost knocked off his feet.

Borrocks swung the weapon again and missed by a whisker. The next time he swung it, Slocum ducked, grabbed Borrocks's single suspender, ripped it down and yanked down his pants. Then, straightening, he slammed him in the neck. Backing away, quicker with his footwork now that he had his second wind, Slocum watched the big man flounder as his pants fell farther down and he tripped.

"That's for the bung starter, you sonofabitch!" Then Slocum feinted and drove a tremendous right to Borrocks's chin, landing him flat on his back on the floor. He was out cold.

Slocum stood with his feet apart to hold his balance, and looked down at the inert vigilante with his legs entangled in his fallen trousers.

"Jesus!" somebody murmured as awe took over the room.

"He is coldcocked for sure," someone else said.

Gulley Tyrone walked over and stood beside Slocum, looking down at the fallen leader of the Regulators.

"He should never have pulled that bung starter on you," Gulley said.

"He should've handed over that belly gun when I asked him nice like," Slocum said.

But it was Cecil the bartender who had the last word. "Some days it's just better to stay in bed."

"The point is, my friends, that John Slocum is a man I can use. I'm finally convinced he's not working with the law. Let me put it even more strongly; the cause needs him."

Clime, an absolutely neutral expression on his face, sat behind his big desk looking at the battered face of Noah Borrocks and the controlled Miles Hammer. They had been in conference for only a short while, the subject being—once again—John Slocum and what was now clearly to be seen, the test of wills.

"He just don't want to do what you want," Borrocks said. "I'd of made the sonofabitch if I hadn't of slipped. But I'll even it with him."

"You agree with that, Hammer" Clime's teasing eyes swung to the sheriff.

"I do. I fully agree with Borrocks. The man was lucky and, of course, there were the customers in the saloon to think about. Otherwise, I'd have handled him on the spot."

"And," Clime added with stern emphasis on that small word, "And not forgetting my orders to *not* arrest him, but to pay out his rope to let him hang himself."

"How do you see that, Hoving?" Hammer asked, crossing his ankle onto the top of his other knee, and giving a quick glance at Borrocks to see that he caught the use of Clime's first name.

Borrocks had taken out a wooden lucifer and was picking his teeth.

Hoving Clime cleared his throat. Good, he was thinking. It was the moment, the mood he'd been maneuvering for, where he could lay down the cards and show them just how it was going to be. No loose ends. Nobody saying he didn't know. And at the same time, no one getting wise to the play. He leaned forward, clearing his throat again, lacing his thick fingers together as he leaned his forearms on the desk.

"Our aim, our purpose—as you realize, both of you— is the establishment of a community here in Bountyville and the surrounding country which will—it is sincerely to be hoped—be a credit to our country, to our fore-fathers, and our children's children, and, above all, a credit to God." He paused, leaning back, still with his fingers interlocked; his eyes dewy, his cheeks heavy with responsibility.

"We have come a long way already; but now there is one more step so that we can feel secure in the face of the wilderness, the savages, and—alas!—the depredations of our fellow whites. We have, as you both well remember, the grim example of what happened at Mountain Meadows; the wipeout of the Fancher train. Such religious ferocity we will not tolerate!" And suddenly he raised his fist and brought it down on the desk. A pencil jumped. The inkwell almost spilled, but didn't.

"No, we will not allow persecution, bigotry, and religious hatred to feed or fester in our community. We are God-loving folk and we will defend to the death our freedom to worship. We are—in a world, gentlemen—soldiers of God!" Eyes closed, the great head bowed before the higher force.

Silence gripped the room.

After a moment, Clime resumed. Now his tone was even, assured as always and, of course, penetrating. The soldier of the Lord had now taken on the uniform of the soldier in the field.

"I heard—as you know—that this man Slocum was on his way north and might very possibly come by here. He had been driving cattle, for Ian McDonald, and that is how I heard this. When this fool of yours—" He glanced suddenly at Borrocks. "—suddenly decided to masquerade as John Slocum, an idea hit me. Why not get hold of the real John Slocum. The man, I'd been told, had ridden with Quantrill, and his exploits are not unknown, though he does nothing to toot his own horn." He leaned forward again, looking keenly at the two men on the other side of the big desk.

"Easton was crazy," Borrocks said suddenly, set- tling deeper into the big armchair. "But he did attract Slocum."

"I daresay the real Slocum would have come here with or without that idiot if he'd a mind to. In any event, Easton's exploits as Slocum seemed at the time to offer a way to put the argument to our man. A little bargaining. And also as the fake Slocum, the real Slocum was further blackmailed. He was now an outlaw—bona fide—in the eyes of the community."

" 'Ceptin' that rankled him 'bout as much as peeing into a hurricane," observed Miles Hammer dryly.

"It brought his curiosity, you dumb shit!" snapped the Reverend Hoving Clime, losing his role, his cheeks coloring. "And that meant we had a rope on him. All we had to do was nub it."

Noah Borrocks sat up suddenly in his deep chair, uncrossing his long legs, and said, "Never heard you using range talk before, Mr. Clime." His face revealed true surprise.

Clime felt most gratified for the opportunity to reply, saying that he had been around a good bit more than some people appeared to give him credit for. And he thought pleasurably to himself how he would savor this later in telling it to Callie, his "pet kitten."

Finding himself again, he cleared his throat, address- ing the seriousness of the moment. "Understand then, that Slocum is most useful to us. In spite of the fact that he has actually done nothing to indicate a criminal nature, he has been arrested and put in jail, he has been involved in a fistfight in the Only Time, and in a confrontation with guns in the Elk Saloon."

"But those were situations that he wasn't causing," Hammer said.

"Doesn't matter. He was there. Innocence doesn't matter when the paint can is thrown at you. People will remember the dramatics, not the truth of a situation. The truth is never interesting, my lads. What is interesting is what you can use, what you can get away with."

"I don't get it," Miles Hammer said. "The man was arrested and you told me to let him go. Then, he was braced by Borrocks here, and now in a way you're saying let him go again."

"You don't understand, Hammer. Now listen carefully. Slocum is useful to us as long as he is mobile. You understand? He hasn't done anything that would really call for an arrest or for the law to get on him. And he very likely won't."

"Then—?" Miles Hammer opened his hands in wonder and looked over at Borrocks, who was quietly, almost imperceptibly shaking his head.

"Then?" Clime's eyebrows lifted, his eyes were bright with amusement. "Then it is very simple. If anything goes wrong; that is to say, goes the way we don't want it to, we have a perfect and very handy scapegoat." He paused only briefly before going on. "Remember, lads, that people always need somebody to blame when things go wrong. That is an ironclad rule of the way human beings behave." He paused again. "Now do you understand what has been going on?"

After a moment of silence, Hammer said, "What if he gets onto it? Sees what's happening, that he's bin fenced in. What then?"

Clime's face was without expression, though there was a slight glint in his eyes as he calmly said, "Why, Borrocks and I have discussed just such a possibility. And so there's nothing for you to be worried about, Miles. Everything—I say everything—is under control."

Miles Hammer was staring hard at the situation, and as Clime finished speaking, he sniffed. It was obvious that he didn't follow what the other man was saying.

"I see you're still puzzled, Miles."

"I am only asking what you plan to do if and when Slocum gets smart to what your game is."

"Our game, Miles. Remember: *our*." Suddenly, he whipped out a red bandanna from his hip pocket, almost as though he was drawing a gun, and wiped his forehead. "It's getting hot in here." When he put the bandanna away, he looked at Borrocks. "And you? You still understand exactly what you will do when I give you the order?"

Borrocks, who had been slouching more and more into the leather armchair, now began to uncoil. He sat up. He said, "I am going to kill the sonofabitch!"

Those words put the room into silence.

"But only when I tell you," Clime said presently, "Only at that time, when it is absolutely necessary to help our program, that is, our establishing here in Bountyville and in the surrounding country, our community. The community of Bountyville!" His large eyes moved from Borrocks to Hammer, and then he leaned forward again and said, "But remember this, and remember it well. Both of you! Nothing is going to go wrong!"

He rode the Appaloosa and she the little blue roan, keeping at a walk past fields of timothy and alfalfa, and Slocum found his eyes returning over and over to those great snowcapped peaks that thrust right into the sapphire sky, and never seemed to get any closer.

And as they rode, those things that he saw and smelled—some grazing cattle, the big butte to the east, the smell of the horses, and of course the girl, her nearness and the way they looked at each other from time to time, touched him and there was something that he suddenly knew again, something of himself, his own presence, that he had forgotten. And he felt especially close to himself.

"That looks like a good spot yonder," he said, nodding to their left. "By the creek there."

"I'm hungry," she said, as they turned their horses in that direction.

They were near the town, within a half hour ride, but they didn't feel anything from the life there. They could have been miles away, Slocum was thinking.

"Are you still hungry?" he asked after they had hobbled their horses and walked to the edge of the creek, where a flaming sun's rays danced on the clear water.

"Uh-uh." Her voice was soft as she turned to him; soft because no thought was given to his question. For both the question and answer had no real place in the present moment.

He had slipped his arm around her and she had already moved farther into his atmosphere, her body sealed to his, as their lips met.

Now, with the sunlit branches of the trees dancing shadows over their naked bodies, they lay in ecstasy; breathing as one, their bodies one movement as he entered her, she guiding his stiff member to its extraordinary desire.

"Am I too tight?" she whispered.

"You're perfect." And again their lips met, their tongues probing as their buttocks, thighs, and legs undulated together. And very gently, they came.

They lay in each other's arms, resting, enjoying each other's closeness as their breaths mingled.

"It is divine," she said. "Thank you."

Slocum was silent.

They lay there, not sleeping, but with no wish to be anywhere else. They were content with their companionship; sharing their pleasure, their freedom, sharing each other.

After a while, she sat up. "I'm hungry."

"So am I."

"Well then, there's our famous picnic. How about it?"

"Did you bring any dessert?" he asked as he sat up and began pulling on his clothes.

"Dessert?" She had her shirt on and her underdrawers, and was holding her trousers in her lap.

"Yeah," he said, catching something different in her tone. "You know, what you get at the end of a meal."

"Ah-hah! I think that can be managed." And her eyes locked with his as they sat there once again immobilzed in their reawakening passion.

"I know some people like to have their dessert first," Slocum said. "I happen to be one of those."

"Glutton, huh?"

"That's right."

"So am I."

He was already slipping off her shirt, while she had taken his upright organ in her fist and was stroking it. Then she was down on it, sucking it deep into her throat, fondling his balls, while he reached down and pulled off her underpants, and sank his finger into her wet orifice. In a few moments she swung her leg across him and lowered her bush right onto his mouth, as she continued to suck and lick his cock into a flaming red wetness while he sank his tongue into her wet slit, tickling her, holding her buttocks, one cheek in each hand, as she pumped up and down and squirmed and gasped in between her long, delicious sucks.

Slocum was sure he would go crazy. Suddenly she gagged on his thrusting organ and drew away, lifting her leg over him again as he came up for air.

"I want you inside!" And she was on top of him, straddling him as his shaft sank up into her, all the way till he hit bottom and she squealed with ecstasy.

They rode each other, with her on top, almost losing him—though not quite—as their buttocks pumped and they stroked faster and faster to the ultimate paroxysm of joy.

In the cool predawn, Slocum lay on his back next to the girl. They had fallen asleep after their lovemaking with their arms around each other. But he had not slept for long. He had awakened while it was still dark and, looking up at the star-filled sky, he had listened to the gentle breathing of the girl lying beside him. His arm, on which she was lying, was stiff, and he managed to remove it carefully without awakening her.

He wanted to think. He needed to think. For pretty soon now he was going to see Clime. And Slocum knew that he would see him on his own terms, not on Clime's.

What was that man up to? Why had he wanted to see him, and why was he so persistent? And just who the hell was Clime? Something, somewhere in his memory laid claim to that name. He had heard it somewhere before. Which was one of the reasons why he had taken his time in replying to the man's invitation. Clime. By now he knew he had picked up all the information and gossip he could possibly get on the man. Which wasn't very much. The nub of it was that Clime was a leader, an adventurer, yes, a man with a mission.

He, Slocum, had known such men. They had opened the West, after all. Some had been useful to the doctrine of Manifest Destiny, others had been simply thieves and mountebanks taking advantage of innocent people— as well as other thieves like themselves—and some had stumbled along, meaning well, but in spite of stupidity or lack of knowledge of the character of the great assortment of humanity that was endlessly tumbling into the great West, had somehow survived, or somehow gone under. Sometimes, Slocum, in a wry mood, would wonder what the Indians thought of this remarkable activity.

In any event, Hoving Clime appeared to be a man who knew which end was up, and even more. And John Slocum was wisely holding his view of the man in abeyance until he confronted him. He had dealt with such men before. They were rare, but he knew that a man could learn something from such an adversary. A man like Hoving Clime tested your mettle. And to be sure, the fact that Clime had clothed himself in the atmosphere—without actually saying so—of the clergy was the touch that told Slocum he was dealing with a master. A lesser man would have claimed right out that he was a man of the cloth. Hoving Clime, on the other hand, insisted that he was only "a humble servant," without any direct authority from either the church or heaven. Yet, of course, behaving as though he really did have that authority, wrapped within the modesty of the acolyte or even the true leader who, to be sure, needed an external authority only as support for the establishment and development of his work on the secular level. A beautiful no-lose game.

But it was still a question that was ringing through Slocum, and getting louder all the time: Was Clime truly what he appeared to be, a man with a mission to help people, to spread the word of brotherhood and build a decent community at Bountyville, or was he out for something else?

To be sure, the man was not all that holy. Slocum understood that without any question, simply judging by the man's actions, and the fact that he was working with such men as Noah Burrocks, Miles Hammer, and presumably the man called Easton, who had pretended to be John Slocum. True enough that many an honest man in helping to build the West and open the frontier had found it necessary to resort to hard measures. After all, it was a rough, tough, even wicked job to push back a frontier and build a civilization. And it required rough and tough men. The point was—as Slocum saw it in the present instance—it all depended on a man's true motives. How personal was such a drive?

Then, too, there was the matter of old Gulley Tyrone. He had grown fond of Gulley, an honest, decent man caught in some action that was by no means clear. Slocum was convinced the man was straight.

Even though Slocum had felt something off about Gulley's insistence on not knowing why the Regulators had been after him, he still trusted the man. He knew his doubt was caused by something related to Annie; Gulley was protecting her in some way.

And his hunch proved a correct one. For it was yesterday that the old man had finally opened up and told him why he was afraid for his daughter.

8

Still lying next to the sleeping girl, he remembered it clearly. He had been feeling closer to the old man, feeling, too, that he might be in danger again, even though Slocum had noticed no outward sign of such a situation.

The soddy had been just as he'd remembered it; the old boy with his endless chew, seated in his ancient chair, and the lingering smell of tobacco, earth, the old logs, and candle wax. And, of course in company with that unique feline-in-residence, Theodore.

There was another chair, which also looked as though it had taken part in more than one saloon confrontation; Slocum, at a nod from his host, seated himself.

"Long time since I seen you about," Gulley said, squinting at his visitor. "Figgered you'd maybe left the country, but then I said no, you'd be the type to hang about to get things settled 'fore movin' on."

Slocum grinned at him. "You're saying I'm nosy, huh?"

"Curious." Gulley sniffed; then he reached to his pocket and took out his little box of snuff. "What you bin up to? No good, I'll be bound."

"I've been trying to figure out the situation," Slocum said. "Wanted to see how you saw things."

Suddenly, he felt something at his leg, and looking down, he saw Theodore's orange fur rubbing against him.

"Bugger makes friends with everybody 'ceptin' him what takes care of him and feeds his fat belly," Gulley grumbled.

Theodore emitted a sound like a meow and continued to rub against Slocum's boot.

Then Slocum decided to take a chance. "I know it ain't my business," he said, "but I'm going to say it anyway—"

"I know what you're going to say; why don't I go see Annie, an' like that. Well, you know damn well why I don't. Now—"

"Wait a minute! Hold it, hold it! No need to stampede it before I even get started." And Slocum was laughing.

In another moment, Gulley had joined him. But then he stopped, and, wagging his head dolefully from side to side, said, "Hell, Slocum, you know I can't risk that."

"But why? What have they got on you that makes you afraid they'll hurt Annie? Now, Goddamn it, I helped you, and you have got to help me."

Old Gulley was staring at him. "Slocum, for Chrissakes, man, I'd say you was the last man in the whole world would need anybody to help him. What kind of shit you handin' me there!"

"I mean a different kind of help, you thick-head. I need to know some facts about this situation in Bounty.

You're the one who could tell me. Why are you holding out on me? I mean it, by God. I'm getting damn all-fired disgusted with you letting this thing—whatever it is— build up to a firestorm just because you don't want to open your mouth. Now, Goddamn it, I am saying it's time for you to tell me what you haven't been telling me."

Gulley sat there with his elbows on his knees, looking down at the floor. His head moved slowly from side to side.

"Slocum, I just dasn't."

"That's bullshit. Hell, I'm about the only person who could help you, you dumb fool. And your daughter," he added, sharp.

The old man looked up, staring at the wall opposite him. Theodore, who had been snoozing a few feet away, now got up and walked slowly over to him and lay down at his feet, but Gulley didn't appear to notice.

Slocum said, "I didn't tell you I met your daughter. I met her at the place where she works."

"You didn't tell her nothin'!" the old man said, cutting his glance quickly at Slocum.

"Cut it out!" Slocum snapped, his tone angry now. "What the hell d'you think I am? Haven't you learned by now you can trust me?"

The old boy was nodding. "I reckon. Just, well, I be a good bit on edge lately. You notice the town's fillin' up with them goddamn Regulators. You know, after what you done to Borrocks, well, maybe you should hightail it elsewhere. 'Course, that's up to you."

"I'm not going anywhere," Slocum said. "Hell, I'm looking forward to meeting this fellow Clime."

"Huh!" Gulley snorted, back into his old form all of a sudden. "Watch yerself with that man."

"I've heard he gives good sermons."

"He does. So, if you want, go listen to him. But sew up your pockets first."

Slocum chuckled at his friend's seriousness. "I will take that advice because it sounds sensible and fits in with what else I've heard about the man."

He waited for Gulley to say something to that, but when he didn't Slocum went on. "People, at least the ones I've heard, seem to figure him as a sharp one. So how come he's running the show if people don't trust him?"

"Oh, they trust Clime all right," Gulley said, nodding his gray head. "They trust him to pinch a silver dollar tight enough to make a hole through 'er. But you see, he's the one who gets things done. Plus, he's got his church, and a lot of the people who might be afraid of him are a whole lot more afraid of burning in hell."

"I see; he's got 'em coming and going."

"Butter wouldn't melt in his mouth, you can bet on it. At the same time, you cross him, it means you're crossin' the Almighty. The wrath of God? You have heerd about it? Yup? Well, the wrath of Hovin' Clime ain't exactly a dewdrop, my friend." He paused to scratch his stomach. "All I can say is, Clime's got his good side and his bad; like the rest of us. Exceptin' his sides is a little sharper than most people got. And he don't stand around waitin' for you to find that out for yourself, if you cotton to what I'm sayin'."

"I'm looking forward to meeting him."

Gulley stared at Slocum, his head canted to one side, one eye squinting to ensure better measure. "Say you met up with my daughter Annie, huh? How is she? She seem all right to you?"

"She seemed fine. And she is also a damn good cook. I recommend that eating place."

"Like her maw," Gully said, his blue eyes looking back into the past. Slocum wondered how old he was.

"Her maw was Shoshone," Gulley added.

"Yeah. I thought I saw Indian in her. She's beautiful."

"That's what I know," Gulley said, nodding his head. "And that's one other reason I keep quiet about me an' her. You know how folks are about such things. She happens—luck—to be light-skinned. I sometimes wondered maybe her mother was a 'breed. She sometimes put me in mind of her being maybe part white."

"Why don't you go see Annie?" Slocum said. "I bet she'd really be happy about that."

"No. Better not."

At that point, Slocum felt the old man close up again.

"You're still afraid they'll hurt her on account of you."

Gulley was silent, looking down at his hands.

"You're figuring—still figuring—that someone or some people around Bounty will get at her on account of you."

"Somethin' like that." The words were almost a mumble, and Slocum had to strain to hear them.

"And you still say you don't know what it is they want from you. You tried to get me to think that, when they put on that hanging party, they were just trying to scare you or maybe some others along with you; but I don't believe it. That's bullshit. We both know it's more than that. And I'm telling you, Gully Tyrone, if you go on like this, something not so good is bound to happen. Because you know same as I do that if there's something they want from you, they will come and get it. And by God, sooner or later they're going to find out about Annie." Slocum waited a moment, and then he stood up, "I'll be seeing you," he said.

But Gulley had also risen to his feet. "C'mere," he said, and gestured for Slocum to follow him across the soddy.

Slocum started to follow him, but then Gulley stopped and turned back toward him. "You know I ain't seen Annie since I got shot off the stage. She look well, did she?"

"She looked fine," Slocum said. "She's good. I liked her right off. You're a lucky man to have a daughter like that, my friend."

"You didn't tell her you knew me."

" 'Course not."

The old man seemed to hesitate. "I wouldn't want that," he said. "You sure you didn't maybe by mistake say anything?"

"I didn't," Slocum said with a smile. Something of the old man now touched him. "Were you going to show me something?"

Gulley didn't answer, but walked to the farthest corner of the soddy. Then he stopped again and said, "Anybody see you comin' here?"

"I don't believe so. I always keep a sharp lookout for such a thing. Especially in Bounty."

"How's the door latch?" And he nodded toward the entrance to the soddy.

"It's good. I checked it when I came in," Slocum said. "You expecting company?"

The old man shook his head. "Just figurin'."

He had reached the far corner of his house and Slocum, who was directly behind him, noticed a pile of sacks and panniers and other articles that, in the dim light, he couldn't quite make out. Gulley had bent down and was moving some of the tarpaulin that was lying over much of the corner.

"This here is mostly diggin' tools," he said. "Pick and shovels, and then these." He pulled out two panniers. They were made of cowhide, and Slocum noted that the straps that would tie the panniers onto a horse or donkey were missing. Gulley handed him one of the panniers. "Take that over in the light there," he said.

The pannier was empty. One of the shovels had fallen over when Gully had picked the container, and now he stood it back against the corner of the soddy.

Slocum carried the pannier over the where the light was better. "What do you want me to do with it? It's empty."

He didn't wait for an answer, but was already peering into the container, and now he reached in and ran his fingernail along one of the inside corners.

"Light's better outside than this here," Gulley said, "only we dasn't try that."

"No need to," Slocum said, looking at his fingernail. "How long have you had this here?" he asked.

"This good while."

"Long, huh?"

"Long time."

"And they know about it. Somebody, anyway."

"They maybe suspicion it. Can't say for sure. 'Ceptin' they know somethin'. They suspicion somethin'. But I do believe they don't exactly know what they're lookin' for."

Slocum was looking squarely at him. "Do they know who? Who to be looking for?"

"I ain't certain on that. See, I used to do some prospectin'. Up around the Miller outfit, and almost up to the Medicine Creek. Now that's where the Regulators got their camp. Near there. Long time back it was."

"You know how to find it, though."

Gulley said nothing to that. And suddenly Slocum cocked his eye at him. "Do you?"

To his surprise, the old man shook his head.

"You don't know where it is? Holy smokes!"

"I don't. I tried to find it again. For the life of me I couldn't. And I can't. I just can't figure where it was."

"But what happened? How could that be?" Slocum asked. He had heard of such happenings, though they were extremely rare. A prospector found a lode, or some of the yellow, and then maybe there was a storm, or Indians, or he fell and hurt himself and so was unable to find his way back because he lost his bearings. But he had never actually run into such a situation before.

Gulley had taken the pannier and placed it back under the tarpaulin and then returned to his chair, nodding to Slocum to do the same. They sat there, the two of them, for some minutes with neither speaking, each taking in the unique situation; Slocum for the first time, while old Gulley Tyrone had lost count of the time he had spent going over it.

The two of them sat there like that for a long time in the old man's soddy, each turning it over in his thoughts, not quite knowing what to do with it.

At one point, Gulley started to speak, telling Slocum that he'd found the mine by the craziest accident.

"Had a jackass with me," he said, carving himself

a big chunk of chewing tobacco as he leaned forward on his bony knees. "Emanuel. Spooky bugger he was, but we got along good enough. I'd known Emanuel a good while, and we'd prospected about here and there. 'Ceptin' now and again, Emanuel took it into his jackass head to act queer. He ran off a couple of times, and I had a helluva time findin' the rascal. Well we was up there by Medicine Creek. And he took off. I was a carpenter in those days and had a hard time findin' work, so I took to prospectin'. I put together a small grubstake, twenty dollars' worth. Borried it from two gents I'd done work for. I got my groceries and borried a jackass—Emanuel, like I said. I'd used Emanuel before when I got the itch to get out of where all the people was. And so the same feller let me borrer him again. And we set out." He had paused to spit, then sneezed, and then blew his nose between his thumb and the knuckle of his forefinger, first one nostril, then the other.

"I recollect how the third day out we come to deep gulch. Mind you, all this was uncharted mountain. Wild. Well, I cooked my supper, what there was of it; then I fell asleep." He paused again, resettling himself in his chair, and then resumed.

"Next mornin' when I woke up, the sun was already high in the sky. Don't know why I overslept. That wasn't so bad. I didn't mind havin' a late breakfast, but then I discovered Emanuel had slipped his tether."

Then, he looked across at Slocum who was listening attentively. "Had flapjacks and fat bacon. Then I set out to find Emanuel. That damn jackass had plumb disappeared.

"Tramped about for a couple hours over rocks, boulders, hard on my feet on account of my boots was worn pretty thin. Then all of a sudden I heerd him brayin'.

He was up top of a steep slope, not easy to get up, but I done it. Steep, hot, it bein' August, and I had to pull myself up in a lot of places, grabbin' holt on scraggly bull pine, or buck brush, and 'course slippin' about in my thin shoes on shale and rubble. Finally, along in the late afternoon I come upon himself grazing easy as you please in a patch of meadow." He stopped abruptly in order to slice himself another chew and popped it into his mouth neat as a whistle.

Slocum, meanwhile, waited patiently. He was used to old-timers taking their time when telling a story.

"So whilst I'm settin' there restin' a mite, and havin' a smoke of my pipe, I just happened to pick up a piece of rock. Well, rock is rock. All right? But this here was damn heavy. So I took a closer look."

He raised his head and looked at Slocum. "Well, you guessed it. It was gold, real gold. I thought for a time there I was gonna lose my mind. I couldn't believe it!" Once again he stopped abruptly, and fell into a deep silence.

A long moment passed, then another. Slocum waited. And at length, he heard a snore coming from old Gulley. But his own snore woke him and he sat up, shaking himself. And then, to Slocum's astonishment, he continued his story as though there hadn't been any interruption.

"But, see, I guess I did go crazy or something, on account of after digging around a good bit and panning in the little crick there, I marked my claim and then set out with Emanuel and went right back down to Bounty—what was called Lords Town in those days. Well, I never told a soul. Well, I did actually, but later. I used to tell my daughter about the treasure I come so close to findin'; I mean, when she was real little, and it was like a fairy tale. But I never told nobody else." He had squinted his eyes then. "Oh yes, those two fellers in the hotel, Miller Holmes, he was like mayor, or something, and the other I don't recollect his name. And I filed claim; showed some dust. But then—"

He stopped again, scratching himself. "Then, then there come up one helluva godawful storm. I mean, you must of heard of the big storm. Closed up all the trails in and out of Lords Town and all over. And then the Injuns hit us to boot. Some of us—the ones that got away, we was lucky. Damn lucky. Miller Holmes—and yeah, I think it was Darcy—yup, Lew Darcy, the two I'd shown my dust to, they was kilt, 'long with near everybody else what didn't get away such as myself."

"And the mine?" Slocum had asked. Although he'd already figured out the answer.

"There wasn't no mine. Not anymore. A avalanche buried the whole kit an' kaboodle. I went back a lot of times tryin' to find it. Some others who'd likely heard somethin' was lookin', too. But the Injuns caught them. And besides, they didn't even know how to begin lookin' for it. I was lucky, I mean about the Injuns. Maybe havin' a squaw wife helped. I dunno."

"Do you know now?" Slocum had asked. "Could you find it now?"

The old man didn't answer. Instead, he reached behind him under an old buffalo robe that the pack rats had gotten to and pulled out a bottle and two mugs. Without a word, he poured.

"We'll drink to Gulley Tyrone's lost mine," he said, splashing a generous amount of whiskey into each mug. "That ain't forty-rod trail whiskey, my lad. It's real whiskey. I bin savin' it. Dunno what for. For now, I reckon." And he took a swallow, gasping it down.

Slocum followed suit, his eyes watering, but the old boy was right. It sure wasn't trail whiskey, the kind that would knock a horse to his knees.

"You're right about the whiskey," he said. " 'Preciate it."

"Likewise," Gulley said, his tone slightly more jovial now.

"So what happened then?" Slocum asked. "Didn't you get someone to help you, something like that?"

"About like tryin' to find a lost fart in a blizzard," the old man said sourly.

"But what you're telling me, at least what I hear, my friend, is that now someone or maybe more than one have gotten wind of your lost mine."

"That is correct." And Gulley Tyrone turned his face full on Slocum and grinned. "I'd like to tell 'em where it really is," he said.

"I sure bet you would," Slocum said with a wry laugh.

Gulley's grin was wicked. "Exceptin' I do recollect one or two markers, though it's likely they're gone, buried now. Like where that little meadow was. You recollect I mentioned it was where I found my jackass, Emanuel. Well, I gave up finally lookin' for it. But I sometimes dream about it. There was a time when I dreamed about it a lot; and I still once in a while do. See, from a certain angle—and I swear by God that it's so—from a certain angle when I walked in lookin' for Emanuel, after I heard him brayin', it was about the middle of the forenoon and the sun was hittin' the top of a peak. Just the highest piece of it, and givin' off a special light. It was like a star, even though it was daytime, I know that sounds crazy, like I was crazy, and maybe I was. But I swear I saw it like that. By golly, I dunno how many times I went back lookin' for that little meadow, climbin' over all the rock that had fallen down the mountainside durin' that big blow. An' I never could find it. Now, well—"

"Well what?" Slocum had asked, feeling that Gulley had been telling him something that was absolutely true, not a dream at all. It had that definite ring of truth, but not the kind of truth that could be proven on a piece of paper, or by swearing to it, but truth that was felt, felt all through.

"You ever tell anyone that?" Slocum asked. "About the sun on the peak. The star?"

"Annie. I used to tell her bedtime stories. I used to tell her that. Yes. Yes, but nobody else." Gulley paused. "But for sure, they began to smell it. Some men smell gold like rats smell a fresh corpse."

"Did anyone ever ask you about the mine?" Slocum asked then. "I mean recently."

Gulley shook his head. "Like I told you, people used to ask me years back. But no one nowadays. Not many know about it, if any. Exceptin'—"

"Excepting those who do," Slocum supplied. And then, lightening up, he'd asked, "What if somebody did ask you now if you knew where it was—I mean even if buried, lost—What would you say?"

A grin suddenly appeared on the gray face as Gulley said, "I'd tell 'em sure, I know where it is. Up Mike's ass!"

9

As he lay beside Annie under the starry sky, with the smell of pine and spruce, and the sweet scent of the girl sleeping beside him, Slocum's thoughts returned to the story Gulley had related about the lost mine. He tried to understand it, tried to see what was really going on.

Slocum looked down at Annie's sleeping face and smiled. It was wonderful; she had the coming day off from her job, and they had decided to spend some time with each other. Slocum lay there, luxuriating in the anticipation of the morrow.

A brief shower hit them in the early morning, before they had gotten up, though Slocum was already awake.

"Isn't it wonderful?" Annie said, jumping up out of her blanket to stand naked in the rain, falling so lightly, with hardly enough body or weight to carry it to the earth.

And yet, as Slocum pointed out, it wasn't drizzle. The drops were distinct, and just enough to freshen the whole area where they had spent the night. And then the sun rose.

"Isn't it wonderful," Annie cried again, as she began getting something together for their breakfast.

He had already built a fire and had the coffee on. She stood again for a moment by the fire, dressed now in her riding britches and silk blouse, her smile almost turning into a laugh of joy as she watched the sky.

"It was never like this back East," she said. "Although it was mighty nice where I was. But if I ever have children, I want them to grow up here in the West."

"Weren't you here at all as a child?" he asked, as he poured some coffee and she started to heat biscuits that they had brought, along with bacon now frying in the skillet.

"Oh yes. Some. But like I told you, my mom died when I was pretty young. So I got sent East. Friends of my dad's took me in. I have a lot of questions about all that. But nothing worrying me." And she was smiling brightly at him.

All the same, he could tell that her childhood, her background, and probably her family history were still big questions.

"So you never knew your father?"

She shook her head. "Not really, I know I was with him when I was small, but I don't really remember. Sometimes I try real hard to remember. Nobody knows what happened to him. He might be dead. He might still be alive. You see, I was sent back before my mother actually died. I don't really remember her, either. But the people that took me in—Aaron and Millie Scanlon— they were real nice. But now, they're dead." She looked across the fire at him, a small smile on her face. "Shucks, I guess everybody's got to die sooner or later."

"I have heard that rumor too," Slocum said agreeably. And they both laughed at that. And then he said, "I'd say, judging by what I see, I'd have to say your parents sure contributed a mighty lovely looking young lady to the world, and your Aaron and Millie contributed a very well-behaved, intelligent, sweet, and wholly agreeable person."

"Your folks, I'd say, did a pretty good job too, Mr. Slocum."

He squinted at the sky, as now the remaining light clouds vanished, and the sun rose clear of the horizon. "I would sure like to continue this conversation, young lady, but I think we'd better pack up. I do believe we're going to have company. I'll just slip over here for a look-see. You get under cover, too."

In the next moment he had crossed the small clearing and, taking up the Appaloosa's reins, he led him into the line of box elders that ringed the little meadow. Just before he disappeared into the trees, he signaled to Annie to stay hidden where she was and continue her packing; then he pointed to his rifle which he was holding in one hand to show that he had her covered.

From the trees, he watched her. Whoever it was coming up the trail couldn't have been someone intent on harm, for he was making no attempt to move silently. On the other hand, the noisy horseman could have been a decoy—an old Indian trick—with someone else sneaking up from another direction.

Suddenly, two horsemen appeared at the edge of the clearing. The first that Slocum spotted was almost naked, wearing a single feather in his smooth raven hair. Following close behind was a white man, a dumpy little man with a great many freckles all over his face, his neck and, Slocum noted, the backs of his hands. The

Indian was leading a packhorse, which appeared to be fully loaded.

The Indian said nothing, though Slocum, coming out of the trees, made a peace sign toward him, and he responded to it. He sat silent and immobile on his pinto pony. His companion, astride a stocky sorrel, waved a small hand with what appeared to Slocum to be goodwill or maybe relief at meeting fellow whites rather than natives.

"My name is Clarence Hooligan," he said. "This is my guide, Flying Feather."

Slocum nodded and introduced Annie and himself. Annie had come out of the trees in answer to his signal.

"I had no idea we would meet anybody way up here," Hooligan said. "It's nice to meet a friendly face or two." He looked over at Flying Feather, who was sitting there like a stone, and indeed, was just as conversational.

"He doesn't speak any English," Clarence said. "I converse with him through sign language." A number of the freckles on of his cheeks widened as he smiled.

"Hunnh! Flying Feather speak good damn English!"

Clarence Hooligan flushed dark red all over his face. "You never told me that, Flying Feather!" he exclaimed. "I thought you didn't know any English. You should have told me!"

"White man want to know all!" He kneed the pinto who took a step forward, then put his right foreleg out and bending, rubbed his long nose against it.

"I am surveying," Hooligan said, deciding to ignore his guide. "I hope we didn't alarm you appearing so suddenly and mysteriously out of nowhere."

"I heard you coming," Slocum said. He looked over at Flying Feather. "But not him."

"Well, anyway," Clarence went on. "This appears to be the place we want." And reaching into his shirt, he drew out a folded paper. "I'll just take a look at my map."

"What are you looking for?" Slocum asked, glancing at Annie, who was regarding the white man and the Indian with a gentle, neutral smile on her lips. Slocum could tell she was sizing them up. The girl was sharp. Not a person to be taken in by the first story she was told.

Meanwhile, Clarence had unfolded his map and was studying it.

Suddenly, Flying Feather said, "There!" And he pointed off to their right. "Over there is big rocks fall."

"Never mind!" Clarence Hooligan snapped, swiftly folding the map. "I know where we are." He nodded to Slocum and Annie, as he grabbed his reins, almost dropping the map but recovering it in time, and then kicked the sorrel into a fast walk toward the place his guide had indicated.

"Looks like you've got a good bit of surveying equipment there," Slocum said, by way of being friendly.

But the freckled surveyor didn't reply. Instead, he simply nodded his head, waved Flying Feather to hurry, and started quickly across the meadow without another look at the two people who watched him go.

Slocum and the girl said nothing more, simply sitting their horses, watching the freckled man and the Indian as they crossed the meadow and disappeared into the trees.

He was suddenly aware of the girl's silence. It wasn't just that she wasn't speaking, but something else. For he was feeling from her the kind of silence that had in it communication. She was gazing with an extraordinary intensity across the meadow, across the tops of the trees, beyond, to the high peaks of the mountain range north of where they were still sitting their horses.

He was about to ask her what she was looking at, but then he saw it.

"It's gone!" she said. "Oh! Did you—did you see it?"

"I did."

"I can't describe it," she said.

"Don't try."

"It—I feel somehow—I don't know—It's gone—"

"Better leave it."

"But—but it was so beautiful." She was looking directly at him now, and there was something close to pleading in her voice.

He didn't answer her. She was still looking at him, and he saw now that she understood.

He saw the tears standing in her eyes, but she made no move to wipe them away.

"Real things don't last," he said. "And if you try to make them last, they vanish."

"Yes, I know." And there was a soft smile at the corners of her mouth. And then she said, "That's strange, that. I wonder how I know that." Then, "But doesn't anything last?" she asked suddenly.

"Everything has its moment, but if you try to make it last, if you try to possess it, you lose it. It lasts inside your heart, not in your head. And so it doesn't last the way you want it to for your usual memory."

She was looking directly at him now, smiling more openly. "Strange that you say that, for even as I asked about it, I knew what you were going to say. You know? I mean in a certain way."

"I know."

"You must know a lot. I feel that about you, that you know a great many things."

"Everyone knows such things," Slocum said. "The thing is, not many of us remember what we really know; we're too busy trying to learn new things."

"Can I ask you something?"

"Sure."

"Did your father teach you these things? I ask because I don't remember my father."

"My father taught me a lot. I owe him. But what you're speaking about came from someone else."

"Oh?"

"An Indian."

"Indian!"

He nodded, canting his head a little. "That's right. An old man. He told me I needed to remember what I already knew, but that which I'd forgotten. So I took him seriously."

She was silent now, and they started across the meadow. When they reached the farther edge, away from the direction in which Clarence Hooligan and Flying Feather had taken, Slocum drew rein and, turning the Appaloosa, looked back at the distant peak on the far horizon.

"I don't want to leave," Annie said after a long moment. "Anyhow, I can't see it anymore."

"I can't either," he said. "But it's there."

Presently, when he nudged his pony, she said, "Thank you."

Slocum was squinting at the sky. "I reckon it's about halfway through the forenoon," he said. And he was thinking of Gulley Tyrone telling his small daughter bedtime stories.

•   •   •

Morning penetrated the valley's silence without disturbing anything, then slowly the light climbed the sheer walls of the narrow canyon that led through to the headquarters of the men known as the Regulators. It took a man a long while to learn the intricacies of passage in and out of the outlaw camp. No one was actually encouraged to develop this ability, for it was secret. Yet, to the extent that it needed to be known by certain riders in order to properly execute their assignments, instruction was permitted. A man was shown—once—how to get in and out on his own. And that was it. All of the men only entered and left the camp when riding under someone's command. Needless to say, everyone learned the rules as quickly as possible.

This morning, the big man had been up in the dark, as was usual with him, and now, as the tip of the rising sun touched the highest rimrocks surrounding the camp, he walked to the big corral to check his saddle horses and to choose the one he would ride that day. Big Noah Borrocks had an uneasy feeling about something, and he didn't know what. It wasn't long before he found out.

He had just finished checking his saddle rig in the barn and had walked outside, when he heard the signal. He touched his handgun at his hip and then crossed the open area outside the barn, circled around, and worked his way through shrub and some deadfall to another clearing enclosed by a large, angular pole corral, which had been used for breaking horses. Lately, the men had been using a different corral for that particular work, one that was sturdier, and the present structure had been left to fall into disrepair. Some of the poles had fallen, and the gate had a loose hinge so that it couldn't close properly.

However, the corral had been granted a second life, since the head man of The Roost, as the outlaw headquarters was called, had found a good use for it. At one end of the enclosure, some limbs had been constructed into a high bench on which were a variety of bottles, cans, and other objects. From the branch of a tree that was hanging over the top rail of the old corral, strings and rope were holding other objects, such as bottles and dummy figures that offered obvious targets, for the place was a practice shooting range. Along one side of the corral playing cards had been nailed, and targets with bull's-eyes and also pictures of men cut from old newspapers. There were also some large drawings—quite ineptly executed—of the human figure—front, back, and profile.

All of these accountrements had clearly been put to good use, as the numerous bullet holes attested. For the leader of the Regulators who now stood regarding this scene had insisted on the practice of the craft upon which the men in his service were engaged.

In this respect, Noah Burrocks was unlike other outlaw chiefs. He insisted on discipline and he insisted on accuracy with all the weapons that the group used. Under their leader's urgent tutelage, the men had become skillful and had learned—though often reluctantly—to appreciate their leader's zeal regarding their education and training.

Noah Burrocks rarely practiced, for he sincerely felt that he was beyond that stage. His reflexes were all that they could or should be, as far as he could tell, and he knew that a man could get tied up in himself by practicing too much. After all, it was the reflexes that counted, the quickness of eye, ear, hand, and body, and especially the ability to pick your own ground, your own time. But lately he'd discovered a growing need in himself to practice his craft, to return to basics.

He had stopped to check his position in relation to a bottle hanging by a string, and a few feet away, a tin can on top of a corral pole. A wind stirred, and he watched the movement of light against the corral gate as a nearby branch moved, throwing a thin, morning shadow.

He heard the second signal from the next guard as the visitor got closer. Well, he'd let them know where he was, and besides, it was a good one to try; the bottle in front, swinging, and then a turn and duck and the tin can.

He checked his holster, checked the light. Don't get the sun in your eyes; don't catch any glint off tin or metal or glass; don't let one single damn thing distract you. Be loose, smooth, and shoot with your whole body, not just your hand.

These were the rules he'd discovered. He'd practiced long, often, under all kinds of conditions. And by God, let 'em say whatever the hell they wanted, but he did, by God, fancy himself—because he was fast, he was accurate, he was here.

For a moment he was still, waiting, saying the orders to himself. Fast, accurate, here. Of course, in real action there was no time for the words, but he would have them. They'd be in his body, in every inch of himself, in his soul. By God, what would old preacher man Clime think of that! He almost chuckled.

Then, shrugging his shoulders to loosen them, moving his fingers, and—the orders. His hand struck; he went for his gun. The bottle, duck and turn, and the tin can.

And by God, he was right here, standing right in his britches!

"Nice," said the voice behind him, as he holstered his gun.

Holding the curse behind his tight lips, he turned to face his visitor. But the curse, though silent, was still there. He'd forgotten the most important part of his drill. The arrival of the unexpected. Somehow—damn it!—in some way he'd let Miles Hammer slip up on him, even though he'd been fully aware just a minute before that the man had passed his guards and was on his way.

But as he nodded a greeting, he realized it had been his lesson. It was plain as a horse knot; he'd lost himself when he'd told himself how good he was. Except, Goddamn it, he was good! He'd bet Hammer couldn't have shot like that! And what about Slocum!

"How about some breakfast? You had a long ride."

"Sure enough."

"Cookie's building biscuits and there's plenty else."

They started walking back down the narrow trail to the large open space where the main buildings were clustered. As they passed the barn, a couple of men leading a broomtail out to the corral, were having trouble.

"Looks to be a tough one," Miles Hammer said.

"The boys've bin sackin' a few broncs," Borrocks allowed. "I believe in good horseflesh."

Miles Hammer chuckled at that. "A man better believe in good horseflesh livin' out here in God's country," he said, and his companion caught the droll humor in his words.

"I see there's a bit of new flesh come in on the yestiddy stage," the sheriff continued. "Heading for Louise's."

"That is always good news," Noah Borrocks allowed, thinking suddenly of the chunky little blonde—Gloria, was it?—who he'd showed a thing or two that last time.

They had just reached the corner of the barn when suddenly a pack rat streaked in front of them.

Miles Hammer started to say something, but before he could speak, Borrocks had drawn and fired.

The sheriff of Bountyville and Lords Town emitted a low whistle. "Damned if that ain't makin' a crowd out of that bugger real fast."

Noah Borrocks stopped, broke his gun, and slipped in new ammo.

"By God," he said, a sudden glint appearing in his deep-set eyes. "That morning poison Cookie's fired up smells real good, don't it!"

"Of course, I know you must realize, Slocum, that the real battle of wills is not the battle that appears to be going on—the one outside, the obvious—but rather, something much more subtle, much firmer, and more complete." Hoving Clime, dressed in black, but without his clerical collar, beamed on his guest, establishing instantly the upper hand in the encounter. Or, at any rate, so he thought.

"Sure enough, Clime," Slocum said, evening it in his use of the other man's name. "Of course, the test of wills is an inner thing. But then, where real things are concerned, there is no such thing as a battle or test of will; there's only what is true, what is real, and what is not." And he beamed amiably on his host.

Clime was quick on the recovery. "Why, I'd no idea you were a philosopher, Slocum. What a pleasant surprise!"

"I am not a philosopher," Slocum said, his tone quite neutral. "I simply say what I see and experience."

"Not what you think, eh?"

"Oh, yes, but the thinking is part of my experience, not bullshit put together to win a point."

"I see you're a self-educated man, at any rate. And more power to you. Even so, you obviously had a formidable teacher at some point in your life. Am I right?"

They were sitting in the dining room in Clime's house, having just had morning coffee with some biscuits, all served by a smiling, totally charming Callie. Slocum had liked her right off, and he said so to his host, as Callie now left the room, closing the door silently behind her.

"You have a charming hostess there, Clime. She knows how to make a stranger feel right at home."

"Thank you. Caligula has had very good training. I do believe in such things."

"So do I," Slocum agreed, and watched the surprise touching his host. Well, two could play at that game, Slocum told himself.

"But I am interested, Slocum, in your way of looking at things. I must say, I am pleasantly surprised, for I'd heard of you as rather a rough, frontier—excuse me—gun type of person. Rather a wrong impression, I now see."

Slocum smiled and said nothing, leaving his host to deal with his material without any assistance from himself.

"Of course," Clime went on, "the frontier has bred and developed some fine minds, along with physical durability and skill. It's what makes our nation great! I am happy to see the fruits of our great country appearing in you and in some others. Alas, it's unfortunate that the poor natives cannot understand the value of a formal, directed education."

Slocum put down his coffee cup and leaned forward. He took a moment to let Clime see his eyes sweeping the room: the furniture, the pictures, the rugs, the fine appointments of a well-to-do home. "Mister Clime, I'd like to say one thing, which is that I wouldn't trade the education of a Shoshone chief or a young boy or girl for all your colleges and universities. Now let's get down to seein' whether or not we can fit this shoe onto this here horse. What do you want?"

"Right now I want a cigar." And Clime reached to the cigar box on the table next to his chair. "Will you join me?"

"No." The answer was quiet, yet firm, and meant no nonsense. Slocum sat quietly in his chair, remembering that Clime had said they would meet in the dining room because he had somebody waiting for him in his office, realizing the clever way the man set up his dealings. Indeed, Slocum found it not only interesting but refreshing. And educational.

Still drawing on his first puff of the cigar, which was clearly a fine Havana, Clime started to speak. "I will get to the point. As you have so ably reminded me, neither of us has a great deal of time to waste." He removed the cigar, coughed gently into his big fist and, with his eyes still on his visitor said, "You asked me what I want. I want you."

"I'm not for sale."

"I know. That is precisely why I want you. Oh, it is not only for me, much as I need a strong, intelligent and—" he made a gesture with the cigar, a hint of a smile in his eyes and at the corners of his mouth—

"resourceful man, but for—" and his forehead wrinkled as his eyes moved heavenward "—for my calling. My purpose here in the West, in Bountyville. Mr. Slocum, you are in the presence of a man with a very, very serious mission."

"And that is?"

"To contribute in whatever degree I am able toward the opening of the West, the conquering of the frontier, of the uncivilized and unholy. I am, sir—I hope you will forgive an, uh, older man's prerogative in saying it—I am, I do believe, a servant of the Lord. I am here in Bountyville to build a church, a school, to bring civilization and the teaching of the Almighty to those who have eyes to see and ears to hear, sir."

He stopped abruptly, sitting back, drawing on his cigar. "Mind you, I am not at all interested in converting you to my ways of—well, my way—I believe that's the best way to put it. But I need help, Slocum. I need a good man! I've studied you. You will pardon me, but I must confess I have been testing you, for I wanted to, as the saying has it, I wanted to test your mettle. And I have, and you're the man I want to handle my work." He paused, holding up his hand so his guest would understand that he had not finished, but was searching for the best approach, the right word. Then, opening his hands, he resumed. "As it stands, I have only time to concern myself with spiritual matters. I need a man to take complete charge of the more secular affairs. And, well, you're the man." He leaned back, picking up his cigar, which he had carefully placed in his saucer. His eyes stayed right on Slocum as he emitted a small cloud of smoke, though toward the side of the room.

"What do you say?"

"Sorry."

"I could make it worth your while, Slocum. Well worth your while."

Slocum was shaking his head, even before Clime had finished speaking.

Silence fell between them. Clime sat in his his chair, regarding his guest from behind his cigar. Slocum simply waited for Clime's clincher. He didn't have to wait long.

Clime took the cigar out of his mouth and leaned forward. His legs were stretched out in front of him as he leaned on the arms of his chair, with his ankles crossed one over the other.

"You know, Slocum, I am doing everything I can to convince you of the benefits of accepting my proposition."

"Such as?"

"Such as remaining a free man."

"I am a free man."

"Are you? You know, there have been so many episodes of lawlessness in our fine town that I am on the verge of taking rather desperate measures."

"I've been expecting it," Slocum said evenly.

"I am glad to hear that, because then it will be no surprise to you when Sheriff Hammer asks the Army to impose martial law."

"That will take some time to go through. You know the Army, I'm sure."

"Meanwhile, Hammer has the full cooperation of his deputies. The men under Noah Borrocks who have had such good experience in wiping out Plummer's bandits up in Virginia City and the country around. They are only waiting for an order from me. I don't really know why they turn to me, I am nothing in that line of work; but perhaps it's because of my rather large constituency.

And so, I do wish you would reconsider."

"You can't get away with that, Clime."

"I'm not bluffing."

"Oh, I know that. You'll go all the way to get what you want."

"And do you think you know what I want, Slocum?" Clime's face had turned almost to a smile of amusement.

"I know very well what you want. You and your kind."

"Be careful how you speak to a man of God!" His tone was suddenly sharp.

"You're no man of God. You're a man of Clime. I know very well what you want."

"Tell me then!" Clime was sitting back, a look of amusement still on his face, but Slocum didn't miss the slight tapping of his fingers on his thigh.

"I believe you've said what you want, Clime. Of course, not in just so many words. You want your empire."

"The empire of the Lord! It isn't mine!"

"That's your cover. But I know very well you're not playing for anyone but yourself. Yourself—and the gold. Didn't your surveyor tell you we met?"

Clime made no response to that.

Slocum stood up. "I think that's enough," he said.

"You could make a lot of money, Slocum."

"I already have a lot more than you, Clime." And he turned and walked to the door. "With his hand on the knob he turned and nodded. "Thanks for the coffee."

Clime was standing. His face seemed to Slocum to have turned slightly gray, but he knew that could have been a trick of the light. There was no trick, however, in what Clime said next.

"Give my regards to Gulley Tyrone, Mr. Slocum."
And his mouth opened slightly, and then he chewed once
on his upper lip as though getting ready for something.
"Oh, and give my regards to your attractive friend. I've
heard that the place where she works makes very fine
coffee. I might drop around."

Slocum felt it hit him right where he was sure Clime
wanted it to hit. He had started to turn the knob to open
the door, but now he didn't. He dropped his hand and
faced the other man squarely.

"I wouldn't advise that, Clime."

Clime's face had broken into a steely smile. "Oh,
there would be nothing personal, I assure you. Nothing
like that. You know. Let me tell you an interesting
detail, at least to me. Some years ago, I studied many
interesting subjects, one of which was anthropology and
another anatomy. I learned something very interesting
and it is this: that very often one can see the physical
similarities in two apparently quite different people not
by studying, as one might suppose, their facial charac-
teristics or structure, but their—would you believe it?—
their backs, especially the nape of the neck. Interesting,
isn't it?"

Somehow, Slocum knew he had been waiting for it.
"It is interesting in one respect," he said as he opened
the door, and half turned back to face the man who was
now standing in the center of the room. "It can tell us
the difference between slime and Clime."

He saw the color spring into the other's cheeks. "Oh?
What is the difference, Slocum? I mean, if you care to
tell it."

"There isn't any."

Slocum closed the door firmly behind him.

10

"So that's set, then."

Miles Hammer nodded, as Borrocks passed him the bottle. They had spent a couple of hours together, going over the plan, the plan that Hoving Clime had suggested for the pacification of an unruly and close-to-being-out-of-control Bountyville.

"When?" Borrocks asked. "The way you were talking, you sounded like he wanted us in there pretty damn soon.

"As soon as possible," Hammer replied. "Like tomorrow. Except, remember, it isn't him who wants you. It's me, the sheriff, the law. You're all deputies. You'll have to give me a list of names in case there's trouble."

"Trouble?"

"Like from the Army."

"Huh."

"Now, you've got the plan. How many men needed in each area. You pick who, 'course. And you and me, we'll be close."

"I got it." Borrocks took another drink. "Good stuff on a nice morning, ain't it?"

"Good stuff on any morning," Hammer agreed with a grin. "It should go easy enough. We just let everyone know the law is taking over and the bandits and stuff will stop or else get shot up or arrested."

"What the hell we gonna do for a living then?" Borrocks grumbled.

"You'll see. Clime has a great plan."

"I'll believe that when I see it. I mean, I'm sure he's got a great plan for himself. But I'm thinking of us. Myself. And my men," he added in a much lower key.

"Everybody is going to be well taken care of," Hammer said. "Clime went over the whole thing closely with me. And I'm telling you just what he said, just what he wants. Shouldn't be a hitch. It's simple as pie."

"Just take over and stop any night work; no hosses, cattle, and so on. Shit, I'd gotten my eye on that little old bank they started up in town there."

"Look, don't you get it?" Hammer was having trouble controlling his impatience. "We lay off and then everybody figgers we've taken care of the road agents, run 'em off, see. And then when everything's relaxed and all, we can hit 'em good. That's how Clime is seeing it. But we have got to play along with him. He's doing a good job pulling everything together. Hell, you know how the pickings used to be; pretty damn piss-poor."

They were sitting in Borrocks's cabin and now the door suddenly opened and a young woman walked in.

"Francey, I always told you to knock first," Borrocks said. "Goddamn it." But he wasn't angry. "C'mere." She walked over to where he was sitting with the bottle in his hand. "Have a drink," he said. Then he turned to Miles

Hammer. "This here is Sheriff Miles Hammer come to arrest me. Hah!" And he broke into a big laugh as his hand began to fondle her rump.

"Francey, go on inside, I'll be free here in a minute."

When she had gone into the other room, Borrocks turned to Hammer. "That it?"

"That's it, except one thing."

"Sure. Slocum."

"You set?"

"Don't worry about it. I'm ready for the sonofabitch."

"That is a definite part of the plan, Noah. I'll be there to help set it up, like we spoke of before."

"I don't want any interference, you understand. Slocum is my meat."

"You got him. I've talked it all over with Clime. That's the way he wants it."

"That's the way I want it," Borrocks said. And he stood up and nodded to Hammer and walked into the other room.

Miles Hammer let himself out of the cabin. He walked quickly to the corral where he had left his horse, tightened the cinch, mounted, and without looking about, rode back out of The Roost.

"That's the way I want it," he said as he pointed his horse toward Bountyville.

The first person Slocum saw who he actually knew after he left Clime's place was Terence. The young man was chipper as he greeted Slocum from behind his desk.

"I heard how you handled that feller in the saloon, Mr. Slocum." Terence's face was shining with admiration and hero worship.

Slocum had been ready to brush him off, hating that kind of thing, but at the same time he had two thoughts: one, he didn't wish to be unkind to Terence, who was a very decent young man; and two, he knew he needed whatever help he could get.

"I want to talk to you a minute. Is it all right here? We don't want to be heard."

"I'll keep a watch on the door, if you'll watch the stairs," Terence said, and he had stepped instantly into the role of conspirator. Slocum knew he could trust him.

"I'm going to need your help, Terence."

"Just tell me what to do, Mr. Slocum."

Swiftly, Slocum outlined the plan that was being hatched for the takeover of the town under the ruse of invoking martial law. "We need to get somebody to ride right now to the Army at Fort Bent."

He saw Terence's face fall.

"What's the matter?"

"I can't ride, Mr. Slocum."

"You don't know how to ride a horse?"

"It's not that. I—I can't. I've got the piles. I don't think I could make it."

"Who could we get? I mean somebody we can trust."

At that moment, as they were standing together at the desk, he saw the skinny girl Clementine who had caused such a ruckus in the Only Time saloon when he'd first come to Bounty. She was coming out of the dining room, and she was alone. But then in the next moment Slocum saw the young redhead who had been her great defender at the bar and gotten knocked cold for his pains, following behind her. Red was jabbering away about something, while the girl was looking over at the two men at the desk.

"There's that man who you were with at the Only Time," she said.

"Y-yes, it-it is," said Red Langley. Slocum remembered his full name now, and the trouble the boy had in saying it.

"Do you know him?" he asked Terence.

"Sure. Everybody knows Red."

Red and his friend Clementine were already coming across the lobby to greet Slocum and Terence, both with big smiles on their faces.

"Maybe you can help me," Slocum said, when everybody had said hello. "It's important that I get a message to the Army at Fort Bent. It's a good ride from here. And Terence here can't go. He can't leave his job." As he said those words, Slocum felt the young man beside him tighten against the possibility of his saying why in front of the girl, and then he felt him relax with relief when he didn't. He wanted to grin at him, but it was definitely not the time for grinning.

"M-me. I—can, can g-go, r-r-ride," said Red, stumbling over his words, shaking a little.

"I can go," said Clementine firmly. "I'll get there quicker than you. A woman wouldn't be bothered. But you, with that red hair, some Indian would favor that for his trophy, I'll be bound!" Clementine all but snapped to attention in front of Slocum. Such was their zeal, their enthusiasm, their willingness to help that Slocum wanted to grin with pleasure. But he realized that what was needed was the stern approach.

"What do you think, Terence?"

"I don't think Clementine should go."

"That is nonsense!" snapped the young lady and stamped her foot and crossed her arms on her chest, high up, almost at her neckline, like she was posing for an artist, Slocum suddenly thought.

"I have an especially important job for you here," he said. "I need a lookout." He turned to Terence. "Can you go down to the livery and rent a horse for Red? That all right, Red?"

"Sh-sh-shure—"

"I'll watch the desk while Terence gets the horse."

"I'll have to lead him up from the livery," Terence said, his face gloomy. "Can't help it. I can hardly move."

Clementine was staring at him, her eyes pecking all over his face, his chest. "I'll get the horse. Leave it to me." And she was gone.

Slocum was just glad that none of them had asked why he'd not sent Red to the livery. He liked that. He liked the way they all accepted the boy's infirmity.

About fifteen minutes later, Clementine was back with a little bay horse.

"You walk out of town with Red," Slocum said to her. "Take your time, leading the horse, like he was seeing you off. Then, when you're out of sight, you come back and he takes off. Here, Red, I've drawn you a map how to get there. And I've written a note for the C.O. there. That's the officer in charge."

"G-g-good." Red was all smiles. "I'll—I'll g-g-go f-fast."

"Main thing is fast, yes," Slocum said. "But also carefully." He thought a second and then said, "Anybody stops you wanting to know where you're going, just say you're trying to get a doctor at the fort. See, you could run into one of the gang and might not know it."

In another minute the pair had left them.

"I feel bad I couldn't," Terence said. And Slocum saw that he did look miserable.

"Cheer up. There's plenty for you to do. First thing is not to let on that anything has happened. Then—"

He paused, sizing the young man up. "You said you wanted to learn something about guns."

"I do."

"Then your first lesson is starting right now. Get somebody to spell you for a few minutes at the desk, let's say an hour from now when I'll be back. And I'll show you some things."

Terence was grinning happily now. "Good, Mr. Slocum. I can get somebody and I'll be looking for you."

"By damn! Why'n hell didn't you get meself to ride, 'stead of that poor kid! He'll get hisself scalped, or throwed, or plumb lost!" Gulley was in sulphuric form as he stomped about his soddy after being filled in by Slocum on his meeting with Clime and his instructions to Red, Clementine, and Terence.

"Take it slow, old friend. Take it slow!" Slocum held up a restraining hand as the old man snorted and cursed and finally stood still in the center of his domain, scratching his rump furiously with both hands.

"Fact is, Red's the best choice to ride to Bent because he is a bit off, and if he gets mixed up in telling someone who might stop him why he's heading up there, they can figure it's because of the way he is. You also overlook the fact—Sir!—" And he held up his hand, raising his voice as the impatient Gulley started to interrupt, "Sir!— that it is one helluva long ride to Fort Bent, even if you don't have piles like Terence, and it takes a damn good lot of strength. Let me tell you that young feller Red, and many other people like him, has got the strength of ten."

"Huh!" The old boy snorted. "Huh! Hah! Maybe—!"

"So it's done and no sense cryin' over it."

"Good enough then. So what we waitin' for? What's your plan for here, for the rest of us? I'm ready! Lemme tell you I am ready to face them sonsofbitches! If they think they're takin' over this here town, they are suckin' wind, my lad!"

They had started out seated in the soddy, though Gulley had been up and pacing back and forth as he delivered his views on the situation, but now he sat down again, wagging his old head, sniffing loudly, and at last reaching for support—a fresh chew. For a moment, it appeared to Slocum that Gulley couldn't decide whether to take snuff or peel a slice. The old boy was that agitated. But Slocum could also tell he was rejuvenated; a war horse by nature. Well, they were going to need all of that and more.

"I don't know how this will open," Slocum said slowly, his voice calm, so that the old man would settle. "I am certain there will be some kind of announcement and then the Regulators will ride in and take over."

"You mean they'll ride in and shoot the town to pieces, that's what they'll do."

"Take it slow, now. Let's think. What would we do if we were Clime?"

"I don't want to be that sonofabitch!"

"But imagine. How would you take over the town? For sure not by shooting it up and getting everybody mad and scared and running around and hiding or acting crazy like. If you had any sense, you'd do everything very quietly and slowly and in the open. 'Course, there'll be plenty that isn't in the open. But the folks won't know that till later when it's too late." He reached into his shirt pocket, took out his makings, and built a smoke as he continued. Gulley Tyrone watched him like a bird looking for a chance to peck at some feed.

"Clime wants two things," Slocum went on. "He wants to run the town as his personal community, his followers, his property. Now—wait a minute!" He held up his hand as he felt Gulley's interruption building. "Goddamn it, wait a minute. I haven't even begun to finish what I started to say. Now shut up a minute!" He rolled the cigarette and licked the paper, and continued to speak with it hanging from his lip as he lighted it.

"And the second thing he wants, just as bad as the first, is your mine. With the town and the mine to run he's got what he wants: his empire."

"Fuck him!"

"No thanks," Slocum said. "And don't interrupt. Clime, like a lot of people, is more than just what you might see, more than what he shows. See, he plays the role of the religious, and for all we know maybe he is a religious person. Inside. Who the hell knows what a man is when he's all by himself. Huh? You ever think of that?"

"I don't know an' I don't give a damn what he is when he is by hisself. He is using them road agents to take over this town and also to get his hooks onto the mine. And I dunno if anybody can even find the place."

"That is for sure. We don't know. But we aren't dealing with Clime having found the mine. We're dealing with him looking for it. He wasn't sending that surveyor out there to find out what kind of feed is there."

"So what if he finds the mine? Doesn't mean he'll be able to work it."

"That's for sure. On the other hand, he's got all that free labor. The Regulators and the towns folk. You see, do you? He wants power, and he figures he'll get it by taming the frontier. The dream; you get it? He'll be a hero, something. But now, let's get down to the nub of it."

"Which is?"

"Where is your claim paper? You filed a claim. Remember? You told me."

"I dunno where the hell it is. Everything got all in a mess after the Injuns hit us that time. The damn claim could be anywheres."

"Would there maybe be a copy at Fort Bent? Or maybe Cheyenne? Or where?"

"I dunno."

The silence that fell was punctuated only by Gulley sucking his teeth and gums. Slocum looked over at Theodore, who had removed himself from the scene during the time of Gulley's interruptions, which were loud and vigorous, and disturbed his rest. Now he had returned, still seeking an agreeable spot for a snooze, or possibly looking for something to eat or drink. Slocum half-watched him. He was thinking about Annie.

"I've got to go now," he said. "I want you to get on over to the Trail Inn. I told Terence to expect you."

"Where you off to? And anyways, I want to stay here."

"They'll come here for you, Gulley. And we need to handle this thing together."

"You got a plan, have you?"

"Just about. Now, stop arguing it and get on over to the Trail. Bring whatever guns and other weapons."

"When d'you think Clime's gonna make a move? We could set over there at the Trail this good while an' he'd be settin' at his big stone house just pickin' his nose or somethin'."

"No, he won't. Besides, I just remembered something important."

"What's that?"

"Tomorrow's the Fourth of July. Wouldn't that be a real likely time for him to start his ruckus?"

His first stop was the Trail Inn, where he was glad to find Terence had a substitute on duty, and so was free.

"When are we going to start practicing then, Mr. Slocum?" he asked. "I'm not trying to rush you, I'm just eager to learn as much as I can as fast as I can."

"Very good," Slocum told him. "Now, the first thing to learn, and to remember at all times, even in your sleep, is to notice everything."

"How do I practice that?"

"You just do it. That's your practice. Notice everything. The way a person walks, the way he holds himself, all the details that make up a person."

"I got'cha."

"That's your first lesson."

He watched, hiding his amusement, as the boy struggled with it.

"And the gun part? Is it all right to ask when we might be doing that? I mean, like I thought if I had to arrange for someone to spell me at the desk—"

"The gun part is almost the easiest part. I know you don't believe so. But I am trying to get that across. Guns are a lot like cards. You play the people in a card game, and also in gunfighting. Study what isn't obvious. Study a man's mood, not what he says or does but the way he speaks, the way he does things. You follow what I'm saying, Terence?"

The young man was looking at him with a puzzled expression on his face. But there was something else.

"Is it all right if I call you Terry?" Slocum asked. "You told me that's what your friends called you."

The boy was suddenly all smiles. "Why, sure. That's what I like to be called."

"That's what I know. And since I've been seeing how you are when I call you Terence and how different when I call you Terry, I see something important. Do you understand now what I've been getting at?"

"Yeah. I do. I sure do." And he was beaming all over.

"Now that's your second lesson in how to handle guns. Though we don't need to number anything. Actually, they're both the same. Pay attention. Pay attention in two ways: to what's outside, and might be taken for granted and not noticed, but should be noticed, and to what's inside. Where is the person coming from? See, the thing is to look twice, that's how the Indians put it. Always take a second look.

They had walked into the dining room, and Slocum ordered coffee. They were the only customers. "You want coffee?" he asked Terry.

"No, thanks."

"Good enough. Because I've got something I want you to do." He lowered his voice. "I want you to get a room here for someone. Annie Gilchrist. You know her?"

"Not real well, but I know her to say hello."

"You know where she works now? She isn't still working at the store."

"She's at Happy Times Eats."

"Go there now and tell her I sent you. I don't want anyone who might be there to see me and her together. You understand?"

Terry was smiling broadly in spite of his efforts to control himself.

"Listen; cut that out. This is serious business, my lad."

The smile vanished; the boy sat at attention. He was obviously remembering his lesson. "I will do it just exactly as you say it, Mr. Slocum."

"Tell her to come over here, and I'll see her here at the inn. But not in the dining room. You get her a room. Her life might be in danger. You got it?"

"I got it."

"And a room for Gulley Tyrone. He'll be coming over. If possible, I want them on the same floor with me, close to me."

"Yessir."

"Better go now. Help her with her stuff. Tell her she has to leave her job even if it's not time yet. Insist. And remember that this, too, is part of your weapon training." He paused. "But don't ever forget one thing. I am not training you or teaching you to be a gunfighter. I'm trying to help you grow up in a good way. You understand the difference?"

Terry looked puzzled for a moment, but then he said, "I—I think I do. I'll give it more thought."

"Good enough," Slocum said. "I'll be waiting to hear from you how it went. Also, let me know when Gulley Tyrone gets here."

The morning broke quietly over the town. The air smelled sweet, as though it, too, had slept during the night and had now awakened refreshed. Slocum was up early, even though he had gone to bed late. His plan for consolidating his friends at the Trail Inn had turned out to be more difficult than he'd thought, though he had anticipated some trouble. First of all, Gulley had objected to his daughter being moved there, for fear that she would be in even more danger than she would have been had she remained at Mrs. O'Brien's.

"You're marking her out, Slocum. They'll notice it."

"It's only for maybe twenty-four hours," Slocum had said. "For the day."

"You sure something's going to happen tomorrow, then?"

"If she's at Mrs. O'Brien's she's still more a target than at the Trail, where there are a lot of people. And the same goes for you."

"You didn't tell her who I was?"

"No. But if you don't tell her soon, then I will. But we'll talk about that later." Then seeing the worry in his friend's face, he promised he wouldn't say anything without Gulley's permission.

It took a while to convince Annie that it was indeed necessary for her to stay at the Trail Inn, maybe for only a night, but maybe two. He had told her that there was the chance of a big gunfight taking place, that some gunmen were bragging about treeing the town. And that such events were always especially hard on the women.

"Anyhow," she said, "I'll be near you. And that might be sort of nice."

Slocum grinned at her. "That sure would. But there's trouble in the air, and I'm afraid I'll be up all night."

"I know. I understand." She smiled at him, and suddenly, as they stood in the upstairs corridor outside her room, she took a little step towards him and kissed him on the cheek. And then she turned and entered her room.

It was regrettable with Annie so close to pass up a delightful evening, but he knew very well the thing a horny man had to avoid was being caught with his pants down.

The morning of July fourth, with the air glistening as he took in the sweep of the plain that started at the edge of the town and ran all the way to the big butte to the south, he thought of her briefly, then put her firmly out of his mind.

He had already checked his weapons. He had positioned Gulley at one of the windows and Terry at another. Then he had dismissed them, telling them they'd just be on call, and when the moment was right, he'd let them know to get to their posts.

He walked slowly along the boardwalk to the Western Café and ordered breakfast. He sat facing the door from an angle, with his back to the wall.

Then he heard the first firecracker, though for a split second he thought it was a six-gun. Not yet, he told himself, not quite yet. But soon. It was going to happen today. He knew it. He would bet his boots on that one.

For, above all, Clime was a man for the dramatic moment. And what with his special morning service, plus the excitement of the fourth, he wouldn't be able to resist making big hay out of the historic moment.

But then, as Slocum nursed his coffee following his breakfast of steak and potatoes, he also realized that Clime was clever enough to maybe go against himself at such an important moment. He might just decide to bring in his Regulators before the parade that everybody was expecting.

When he left the Western Café, the street was still nearly empty. He went quickly down to the livery and saddled the Appaloosa and bridled him carefully, talking to him. He led him up Main Street and wrapped his reins once around the hitching rail in the back of the Trail Inn, using a horse knot that he could free with one pull. He alerted Gulley and Terry to be on the watch at their posts. Then he crossed the street and walked down the boardwalk to the Only Time.

There were a few customers in the place, mostly old-timers in the wooden chairs, leaning against the back wall. There was a dealer setting up his faro bank and four men sat around a baize topped table playing draw poker. Big Cecil was in back of the bar, and he gave no sign of recognition when Slocum walked in.

But as Cecil brought a bottle and a glass, which Slocum hadn't ordered, he gave a flicker of his left eyelid and a vague nod of his head. Like certain veteran bartenders in the trade, Cecil could pass on a message without moving his lips. This he did, indicating that there were men in the back room, and that more could be expected from the street.

He leaned forward slightly now, wiping the bar where he had spilled some of the whiskey as he poured it into Slocum's glass.

"Any time now," he said. And moved away, wiping as he went.

"Got any water?" Slocum asked.

"Got'cha."

Slocum saw that no one was looking in his direction, but even so he was being cautious. As Cecil appeared with a glass of water, he spilled some and again took his time wiping up in front of Slocum. "It'll be Borrocks. By now everybody's got the news."

"That's what I figure," Slocum said. "Everybody knows there's martial law."

"And you're packing hardware," Cecil said.

"You are correct, my friend."

"They'll be expecting that." He nodded to the whiskey. "It's on the house. You bin good to Red. He's my nephew."

Slocum nodded in appreciation. "I don't want to drink it now," he said. "So save it for me."

Cecil looked right at Slocum as he picked up the glass and said, "It'll be right under the bar here."

"Good enough." Slocum straightened up, dropping his foot from the bar rail. "Don't want to mess up your saloon, so I'll be headin' outside."

"Watch the rooftop above here."

"Got'cha."

In a few strides he was at the batwing doors and carefully placed his hands on them. He already had Gulley covering the roof above the Only Time from the Trail Inn across the street. Also both Gulley and Terry were covering the entrance to the Only Time in case somebody from the saloon followed him out for a shot in the back.

It was the best he could do. He was counting on Borrocks's rage at the whipping he'd given him, plus Borrocks's obvious arrogance in wanting to be top gun by eliminating Slocum. Slocum was the obstacle that stood in the way of Noah Borrocks claiming to be the fastest gun, whatever the hell that meant.

As he put his hands on the swinging doors, he could hear the noise starting at the far end of the street. It was clearly a band of horsemen, holding their mounts in check before they would ride through Main Street and eventually the side and back streets, making their sweep with the news that law and order were now established.

But the true drama lay ahead in the confrontation with Borrocks. He knew the outlaw mind as well as anybody. And Borrocks was one of the best leaders, and most notorious after Henry Plummer that a man could name. The task seemed easy. And it was. Except for the fact that he was pretty damn sure Borrocks wasn't going to face him without some backup. Maybe the waiting horsemen were that backup.

Luckily, the sun was not directly in his eyes as he stepped out onto the boardwalk. A small cloud had sailed across the sky and was blocking out the direct glare of the sun for just long enough for him to cross the boardwalk and get down onto the street. It was essential to get onto something solid, and it flashed through his mind how he should tell Terry that.

"Slocum!"

Borrocks was coming out of the mortuary not quite directly across from the Only Time, just three doors down from the Trail Inn.

Both of them dropped onto the dirt street at the same time. "You're under arrest, Slocum. Hand over your gun."

"Who says so?"

"I say so, as head of the deputized Regulators."

"Where's the sheriff?"

"Reckon you don't hear me, Slocum. I'm his deputy. Now, either hand over your gun—drop it in the street— or hit leather, mister."

They were facing each other now, and suddenly Slocum caught the sparkle on the roof across the street as someone with a hand mirror was shining it so that he had to move or get blinded.

"Johnnie, don't do that with the mirror!" Borrocks shouted. "I want to take the sonofabitch in a fair draw."

For just that second or two, Slocum's attention was drawn to the man on the roof with the mirror, though he still had his eyes on the man in front of him. He saw Borrocks's eyes glint and was already striking for his gun. It was in that movement that he saw another gunman in the alley across the street.

Slocum felt the tug at his left arm as the bullet creased him, and he knew his hat was hit when it flew off his head. But he had already pumped the ultimate shot into his adversary and, as Noah Borrocks pitched to the street, Slocum had spun a quarter turn and shot Sheriff Miles Hammer right through the heart.

The silence that followed the shooting was louder than the gunfire. The town suddenly froze as the two men lay dead in their tracks.

"Jumpin' Jehovah!" shouted Gulley as he came hurrying up to Slocum, who was rubbing his arm where he'd been creased. "You got a gun arm quickern' a striking snake. Two of 'em!"

"Their little trick with the mirror almost worked," Slocum said as Terry walked up to him.

"They were trying to blind you," Terry said.

Slocum grinned at that. "No, it was more than that."

"How do you mean? They did try to blind you."

"They had a twist to it," Slocum insisted. "See, they didn't have a very strong mirror. In fact, it was probably a piece of tin. No, they were trying to make me think that it was a mirror, and then realize it wasn't, and then—and then—"

"I got'cha. Wow!" Terry's eyes were almost popping with excitement as he realized the game. "That's what you were telling me! They get your attention, and you start to think—and—"

"And they got you," Slocum finished.

In the next moment, he was looking at Annie.

"You look like you don't have a hair out of place," he said, smiling at her, as the crowd began to gather. "Let's get out of here."

Her eyes were shining. "Can I bring my dad along, just for a cup of coffee?"

"Yer damn right you can," said Gulley in no uncertain voice. "But I ain't stayin'. I'll stick for a few minutes, then I got to get back home and see how Theodore's doin'."

"What's going to happen about Mr. Clime?" Annie asked later in the day as they lay in bed at the Trail Inn. "Will he be arrested or something?"

"Depends on how the law sees it. But the Army is due and, while it isn't a military affair, I'm sure they'll listen to the evidence on the situation and will act accordingly."

He rolled over off his back so that he was facing her. They had made love and were both just slightly warm, with a light film of perspiration on their bodies.

"That sure feels good," she said when she touched his chest. "You got me all hot, too."

"Well, we want to be careful neither of us catches cold, lying here by the open window."

"What do you recommend, sir?"

"This." And he pushed his rigid member between her legs, which parted instantly to receive him.

"Would you like to spend the rest of the day in bed?" he asked.

"I can't think of anything better to do, sir."

"I can."

"Yes? What?"

"Spend all day and all night as well."

"And all the next day, too?" she asked in his ear.

"And all—" But Slocum never finished the sentence. Because as he told her—maybe it was the next day—a man who wanted to survive in the frontier had to make sure he paid close attention to what was at hand, not get lost in anticipation of what might be coming down the trail tomorrow or the day after, or after that.

WESTERNS!

at least a savings of $3.00 each month below the publishers price. Second, there is never any shipping, handling or other hidden charges—Free home delivery. What's more there is no minimum number of books you must buy, you may return any selection for full credit and you can cancel your subscription at any time. A TRUE VALUE!

Mail the coupon below

To start your subscription and receive 2 FREE WESTERNS, fill out the coupon below and mail it today. We'll send your first shipment which includes 2 FREE BOOKS as soon as we receive it.